"I am quite shamelessly compromising myself by being out here all alone with you."

"...es, you are. *And* with a man who has no ...mory of you," Nicholas reminded her.

...avinia tilted her head back and gazed into ...is eyes. "He may have no memory of me ...om the past, but has he no thoughts of me in ...e present?"

...icholas looked at her with an expression ...kin to wonder. "You are in my thoughts ...onstantly. In fact, I'm surprised there's room ...r anything else. I wake thinking of you, I go ... sleep thinking of you, and when we are ...gether like this I am filled with a sense of ...eace that pushes away all the uncertainties, ... the pain. You are a part of me, Lavinia, and ...at frightens me."

...rightens you?" Lavinia searched his face. ...ut why, my darling? Why would that ...ghten you?"

...Because if I were to lose you now, I think I ...ould be far worse off than a man without a ...emory. I would be a man without a heart."

Originally hailing from Pembrokeshire, **Gail Whitiker** now lives on beautiful Vancouver Island on the west coast of Canada. When she isn't indulging her love of writing, you'll find her enjoying brisk walks along the Island's many fine beaches, or trying to catch up on her second love—reading. She wrote her first novel when she was in her teens, and still blesses her English teacher for not telling her how bad it really was.

Recent novels by the same author:

A MOST IMPROPER PROPOSAL*
THE GUARDIAN'S DILEMMA*
A SCANDALOUS COURTSHIP
A MOST UNSUITABLE BRIDE

*_The Steepwood Scandal_ mini-series

A PROMISE
TO RETURN

Gail Whitiker

MILLS & BOON®

First published in Great Britain 2006
Harlequin Mills & Boon Limited,
Eton House, 18-24 Paradise Road, Richmond, Surrey TW9 1SR

© Gail Whitiker 1994

ISBN 0 263 84643 1

Set in Times Roman 10½ on 13 pt.
04-0406-60470

Printed and bound in Spain
by Litografia Rosés S.A., Barcelona

A PROMISE
TO RETURN

CHAPTER ONE

"YOU WANTED TO SEE ME, my lord?"

The war minister looked up at the gentleman standing calmly in front of his desk and gruffly cleared his throat. "Yes, Longworth, I did. Sorry to call you in on such a dismal day."

Nicholas Grey, Viscount Longworth, smiled briefly. "That's quite all right, sir. I assumed it was important."

Lord Osborne sighed. "Yes, I'm afraid it is. Damned important, in fact." The war minister laced his fingers on the desk in front of him and took a deep breath. "We have reason to believe that Jean Leclerc is preparing to flee France, and that he is intending to come to England."

Longworth's expression never changed. "Are you certain?"

"All indications seem to point to it."

"I see." Nicholas glanced down at the crudely drawn sketch laying on top of the war minister's desk. "Is that him?"

Lord Osborne sighed. "I believe so, though no

one seems to know exactly who he is or what he looks like. I swear the man has the ability to change form. Every time I think we have him, he slips through our fingers like a tom-cat through an alley gate. All we know for certain is that wherever he goes, he leaves behind a trail of dead British agents.''

''And now he's planning on coming to England.''

''So Baker informed us just before he…''

Osborne didn't finish, and Longworth nodded. ''Yes, I was sorry to hear about Baker. He was a good man.''

''They were all good men, damn it!'' The war minister leaned forward in his chair, his broad shoulders sagging under the weight of his guilt. ''The war is almost over, yet here I am, still trying to track down their killer—a man who has caused me as much grief as Bonaparte himself.'' He stared down at the crumpled, yellowed piece of paper in disgust. ''God knows, I can't risk Leclerc's coming to England.'' Osborne raised heavy eyes to Longworth's face. ''That's why I asked to see you, Nicholas. Under any other circumstances, I wouldn't even suggest it, but there is simply too much at stake not to.''

''Too much at stake,'' Nicholas repeated softly. ''That was the excuse you used for not allowing me to go to France to rescue Lavinia Duplesse, remember?''

"Yes, I do. Unfortunately, this is an entirely different matter. The circumstances make it far more dangerous.''

"Are you asking me to go, sir, or ordering me to?'' Nicholas enquired with an engaging smile.

Osborne ruefully shook his head. "I'm certainly not ordering you to go, Nicholas. I don't even feel I have the right to ask you, after everything you have already done for England. God knows, you have gone above and beyond the call of duty several times over.''

"And yet, you're afraid that if I do not go, there is a good chance that this murderer will be allowed to run free.''

"Yes, but on the other hand, if you do go to France, there's an equally good possibility that you'll be shot.''

A flicker of amusement appeared in Longworth's clear blue eyes. "I hardly think so, sir. As you said yourself, the war is almost over. No one is going to be looking for me any more. The memory of my last mission will have long since been forgotten.''

Osborne raised one grizzled grey eyebrow. "I'm not so sure about that, Longworth. French Intelligence is hardly likely to forget the man who helped

Edward Kingsley to escape. Need I remind you that it was Kingsley's information that played such a large part in undermining Soult's counter-offensive in the Pyrenees? Besides, just because the war is in its last days doesn't mean Leclerc will be ready to concede as well. He's a vicious man, Nicholas. You've seen how he works. He's a cold-blooded killer with no morals and no conscience.''

''All right then. If you're hesitant about sending me, who else are you considering?''

Lord Osborne cleared his throat. ''I have a number of qualified agents.''

Longworth regarded the files on top of the desk. ''Are those the candidates?''

''They are.''

''May I?''

At the war minister's nod, Longworth fanned the folders out on the desk's surface. He glanced briefly at each of the names. He had no need to look at the information within. ''You're wasting your time, my lord,'' he said quietly. ''None of these men is capable of carrying off the mission, and you know it.''

Osborne grunted. ''Perhaps not, but if you refuse, one of them is going to have to try.'' He swept the folders back into a neat pile. ''The only other men I would consider sending are unavailable to me.''

''I take it you mean Edward Kingsley and the Earl of Marwood.''

Lord Osborne nodded. ''Kingsley doesn't even bear discussing. His face is too well known. He'd be shot the moment he set foot in France. And with Marwood away on his wedding trip, that leaves only—''

''Myself.''

Osborne breathed a long-suffering sigh. ''Yes, I'm afraid so.''

Nicholas stared at the painting of a horse on the wall behind Osborne's desk. It was an exceptionally fine Stubbs, not unlike the one in his own library. ''When do you want me to go?'' he asked quietly.

Osborne didn't know whether to look guilty or relieved. ''Are you sure about this?''

''Quite sure. In fact, when you think about it, it's only fitting that I do go.''

Lord Osborne sighed. ''Yes, you certainly have ample cause for wanting to find Leclerc. Given that he was responsible for François Duplesse's death, I can understand your wanting revenge for his widow's sake—''

Longworth shook his head. ''This has nothing to do with revenge, my lord. You and I both know that Leclerc, for all his French name, is rumoured to be part English, and that when the war ends he may try to take his place in London Society. We also know that he will continue to be what he has been for the duration of the war—a murderer.'' Nicholas's firm mouth tightened. ''Or have you forgotten the contents of the missive intercepted before Baker was killed?''

''I've not forgotten,'' Osborne snapped. ''Why in blazes do you think I fear so much his returning to England now? He made his plans for dispatching certain British agents—whether it was during the war or after—very clear.''

''Then is it not worth the risk to send me?'' Nicholas replied softly. ''You said yourself only three men are capable of doing this job, and of those three, I am the only one available to go.''

''Yes, I know that, but there are...extenuating circumstances.''

''What? You mean because I am one of the men Leclerc has sworn to kill?''

Longworth could tell by the anguish on the minister's face that he had stumbled upon the true reason for the man's misgivings.

''That missive was supposed to be confidential, damn it!'' Osborne growled.

''Yes. So was François Duplesse's affiliation with the British government, but someone obviously found out about that," Nicholas pointed out drily. "It seems to me that if Leclerc knows I'm in France, he'll come looking for me. It may be the only way to draw him out, my lord." He indicated the files on Osborne's desk. "He won't trouble himself for any of those men. You know that as well as I do."

Osborne sat back in his chair and studied the reserved face of the man in front of him. "And what happens if you fail, Longworth?"

One dark eyebrow lifted in amusement. "Do you really think I'm going to make it that easy for him?"

"No. If I thought that, I wouldn't have bothered bringing you in. But if you do fail, what am I supposed to tell your fiancée and your family?"

"There will be no need to tell them anything, my lord, because I don't intend to fail."

"But if you do?" Osborne repeated, needing to stress the danger of this mission one last time.

There was a slight pause, before Longworth's mouth eased into a smile. "If I do fail, you can at least be comforted by the knowledge that you won't have to send another man in to find Leclerc. If I do not make it out of France alive, it will be because I'll have taken Jean Leclerc with me!"

LAVINIA DUPLESSE GLANCED at the outrageously low neckline of the tissue-thin gown the modiste held up for her inspection, and arched one eyebrow. "Gracious!"

Beside her, her seventeen-year-old stepdaughter, Martine, smiled in understanding. "*Oui,* it is a trifle…revealing, is it not?"

"Yes, it certainly is. Madame Fouché, can you show me something a little more…discreet, perhaps?" Lavinia asked tactfully. "This is for my betrothal dinner, after all."

"But zis is 'ow zey are wearing zem in Paris, my lady," the sharp-eyed Frenchwoman replied, clearly startled by her customer's request. "And given zat you are ze widow, zer is no need for…'ow do you say *la modestie?*"

Lavinia carefully hid her amusement behind a courteous smile. "It may be how they are wearing them in Paris, *madame,* but I doubt I should receive a very warm welcome from hostesses here in London wearing such a gown. I own, I am more respectably covered when I am in my nightdress."

The modiste sniffed as emphatically as she dared and clapped her hands. "Josette, bring me ze bolts of blue, yellow and rose-coloured silk. Quickly now. And more fashion plates. *Not* ze Parisian ones," she added pointedly.

Lavinia smiled. "Thank you, *madame.* Under any other circumstances, I myself would be in-

clined towards the Parisian styles, having spent as
much time as I have in France. But as I will be
marrying a rather…traditional Englishman, I think
it better that I maintain a proper British sense of
decorum.''

Slightly mollified, the modiste nodded her understanding of the situation. ''But of course, my
lady. And it is an indication of your own refine-
ment zat you would consider ze sensibilities of others before your own beauty.'' She sighed dramatically. ''Such a pity. And such a waste. *Tiens,* we
shall try again.''

Shortly, Josette reappeared carrying the requested bolts of silk, along with a set of considerably more conservative, though equally stylish,
fashion plates. ''Now, I am sure one of zese styles
will be more suitable to a lady planning her second
marriage,'' Madame said optimistically.

Lavinia leisurely thumbed through the plates before stopping at one in particular, her eyes bright-
ening. ''Yes, this one, I think, *madame.*''

Madame studied the plate and duly nodded her
approval. ''*Oui,* very flattering, my lady.''

Lavinia held out the plate for her stepdaughter's
inspection. ''I think it will garner a more cordial
reception from Nicholas's mother than the other,
don't you, Martine? The Dowager Lady Longworth is such a stickler for propriety.''

At the thought of the frightfully upper-crust matron who was to become Lavinia's mother-in-law, Martine nodded. "I am sure she will be much 'appier with this gown, *maman*."

"Good. Now, as for ze colour and ze material?" The modiste pulled forward the fabrics. "Any of zese will look lovely with my lady's wonderful complexion and dark hair."

Lavinia regarded the dainty, pastel shades with a degree of ambivalence, before sliding a thoughtful look towards Martine. "Which colour do you like, Martine?"

Martine's fingers went automatically to the bolt of silk the colour of wild roses. "This one."

Smiling, Lavinia nodded. "Yes, I thought that might be your choice. Madame Fouché, we will have the design we discussed for Miss Duplesse in the rose-coloured silk."

Martine beamed her pleasure. "*Merci, maman*, you are very good to me."

"Nonsense, it is only what you deserve. Now, as for myself…" Lavinia glanced over the collection of pretty pastel fabrics again and shook her head. "No, none of these. Something brighter, I think. Something more…dramatic."

Something befitting a five-and-twenty-year-old widow who is just out of black gloves and ready to start her life again, Lavinia felt like saying.

The modiste deliberated for a moment, and then slowly, a smile began to appear. "But of course, I 'ave it! Josette, *le satin.*" She turned back to her client. "I believe zis will be more to your liking, Lady Duplesse."

And it was. Lavinia caught her breath as the shop assistant returned with a bolt of heavy, lustrous satin the colour of polished sapphires.

"Oh, *c'est magnifique!*" Martine breathed.

The modiste nodded. "And with your colouring, my lady, it will be perfect. See 'ow it looks."

Lavinia carried the length of material towards the glass and held it up to her face. There was certainly no doubt that the colour suited her. The rich, jewelled blue seemed to enhance the radiance of her complexion and deepen the natural blush in her cheeks. Was this how Nicholas saw her? Lavinia wondered, silently studying her reflection.

"My lady?"

"Hmm?" Belatedly, Lavinia realized that the modiste was trying to get her attention. "Oh, excuse me, *madame,* I was…lost in thought."

She turned, and in doing so, found Martine's gaze on her. "It is lovely, is it not, Martine?"

"It is, and you will be the most beautiful lady in London when you wear it," Martine replied proudly. "But then, you would always be that."

Lavinia felt a warm rush of love for the girl who

had become more like a true daughter than a step-daughter to her. Martine Duplesse was as opposite from François as it was possible for two people to be, and at times it was difficult to credit that they had indeed been father and daughter.

At seventeen, Martine was a slender wisp of a girl who had somehow managed to come through the years of the war untainted by the fear and hate that had so permeated France. Sequestered behind the walls of the Château Duplesse, she had remained apart from what was going on outside, until finally, the ugliness of war had reached into their own lives and jerked them from their complacency.

When her husband had been killed, Lavinia had known that neither she nor Martine would be safe any more. Lord Osborne, head of British Intelligence, had sent word to Lavinia to leave Paris immediately. There had been no time to do anything but grab a few of their most precious belongings and flee to the safety of the country.

Lavinia had eventually managed to secure passage to England for Martine with some close friends who were returning to London, promising the girl that she would follow as soon as she could. But as the days turned into weeks, and the weeks into months, Lavinia truly began to wonder whether that would ever come to pass. Her life had become a series of carefully orchestrated moves in a constant attempt to stay ahead of the French. She had gone into hiding, travelling from one small village to another, living as frugally as she could and taking care to avoid the watchful eyes of the French spy network.

Lavinia did not know who had murdered her husband. She only knew that François had been secretly working for the English government, and that someone had stumbled upon the truth of his identity.

Thankfully, however, all of that was behind her now. The months of running and hiding and scraping out an existence as best she could were over. She was back in London, happily reunited with her stepdaughter and comfortably settled in a lovely house in a modest part of town. What's more, she was engaged to marry the man she had been in love with from the very first day of meeting him all those years ago. She had her whole life in front of her.

"Yes, *madame*, this will be perfect." Lavinia carried the length of fabric back to the table and set it next to the design she had chosen. "Now, both gowns must be ready by next Wednesday. Do you foresee any problems?"

The modiste shook her head. "Not in ze least, my lady. In fact, you may expect both gowns by ze beginning of ze week. You 'ave my word."

The selection of their gowns for the betrothal dinner completed, Lavinia and Martine rose and made their way back to their carriage. Lavinia breathed a sigh of relief. "Well, that is one more thing taken care of. Are you pleased with your gown, Martine?"

"Oh, yes, *maman*, it will be beautiful," Martine exclaimed with pleasure. "Everything is perfect, *non?*"

Lavinia tenderly studied the elfin face beside her. She had not expected to be welcomed by François's daughter so easily. Before they'd married, François had told Lavinia of the closeness that had existed between his daughter and her mother, and had warned her that Martine had taken her mother's death very hard.

Moving into the role left vacant by such a woman, Lavinia had felt her own inadequacy most painfully, and had prepared herself for the worst. What she had found, however, was a young girl starved for love and eager to accept the warmth Lavinia was so willing to give. She had been touched when Martine had begun calling her *maman*, and had found the warm bond of friendship that had sprung up between them a heartwarming change from François's quiet, brooding ways. As far as Lavinia was concerned, Martine's love was the only good thing to emerge from the disastrous

marriage Lavinia's drunken father had arranged
for her.

"You are a brave girl, Martine, and I am very
proud of you. François would be proud, too." Lavinia hesitated a moment. "Are you sure you will
be happy living with Nicholas and me after we are
married? I know how much you loved your father."

Martine's expression clouded. "Yes, I did. But
I think that perhaps Papa was not always…an easy
man, and that there was much sadness in your marriage. But when I see how happy you are now, I
cannot help but be glad. And as long as your Lord
Longworth does not mind living with me," the girl
said in her softly accented voice, "I shall be 'appy.
I do not know where else I might go."

Lavinia reached across and patted the girl's
hand. "There was never any question of you going
anywhere else, Martine. You are my daughter now.
I just wanted to know that you would be happy
living in Nicholas's house. Although," she added
with a smile, "if you meet a handsome young gentleman at court this Season you may find yourself
setting up your own establishment before the end
of the year. I was not much older than you when
I married François."

"Yes, but yours was an arranged marriage,"
Martine said with surprising insight. "I would like

to find a gentleman with whom I fall in love and marry because I want to be with him, rather than because I have to be.''

Lavinia nodded, her thoughts returning pleasantly to the man she was about to marry. Yes, she wanted to be with Nicholas. How many times during her unhappy marriage to François had she thought about Nicholas, dreamt about him. Her lips curved in a secretive smile. Her wicked, loving dreams—that's what she had called them. And oh, the hours she had spent indulging in them. At times they were all that had kept her going.

''You are very much in love with Lord Longworth, are you not, *maman?*''

Lavinia blushed in spite of herself. ''Yes, very much, Martine. He is a wonderful man. I know you will think so, too, once you come to know him better.''

Martine considered that for a moment and then shook her head. ''I already know all I need to know about him. I see how happy he makes you. That is all that matters, *non?*''

IN AN ELEGANT TOWN HOUSE in Mayfair later that same evening, the Dowager Viscountess Longworth studied her only son across the length of the elaborately set dining-room table and frowned her displeasure.

"What do you mean, you are going away again, Nicholas?" she enquired sharply. "How can you even consider leaving London at a time like this? Need I remind you that you are betrothed?"

"Mother, I—"

"You cannot simply take it into your head to up and leave just because the fancy strikes you. You have responsibilities, Nicholas. Obligations. You must start acting the part of a soon-to-be-married man."

Nicholas took a sip of his wine and waited for his mother to finish. At sixty-two, Lady Longworth was a regal-looking woman—and as imperious as ever. Her silver hair was neatly arranged under her dowager cap, and while her eyes might not be as bright a blue as they'd once been, they still burned with the fervour that had so characterized her younger life.

"Nicholas, are you listening to me?"

Nicholas brought his own deep blue eyes in line with hers. "Yes, Mother, every word."

"Then why did not you answer me?"

"Because I was not aware you had asked a question for which an answer was expected."

The viscountess bristled. "I will not have you being impertinent, Nicholas. I am your mother, after all."

Nicholas sighed. "Yes, I am very well aware of that. Now, what was it you asked?"

"Humph, I do not know that I should bother repeating it if you cannot have the decency to listen to me the first time."

Nicholas quickly bit back the retort that sprang to his lips and glanced instead at his mother's long-suffering butler, signalling for a refill. "Needless to say, I should like to hear it, if for no other reason than to assuage my curiosity. Ah, thank you, Mortimer."

Lady Longworth glanced sharply at her son's glass. "You're drinking more than you used to."

"On the contrary, I am drinking less."

She studied his face intently. "You're not looking well. Are you eating?"

"I have a competent cook, and dine out at my club at least three nights a week."

"Humph. You probably do not get enough sleep." She slanted him an accusatory glance. "No doubt you are out with *that* woman all hours of the night. I might have known that you would—" Abruptly recalling the presence of the butler, Lady Longworth waved her hand dismissively. "Leave us, Mortimer."

The butler bowed and thankfully made his escape.

Longworth swirled the wine around in his glass.

He'd been wondering how long it would take his mother to get to her favourite subject—namely, the unsuitability of Lavinia to be his wife.

Nicholas knew that his mother had never approved of his relationship with Lavinia, calling her "that immoral Frenchwoman," even though he had taken pains to point out that she was every bit as English as they.

"I am not out with Lavinia until all hours, Mother," Nicholas said patiently. "She is but recently returned to Society after her period of mourning and is well aware of the edicts governing a widow's behaviour."

"Humph." Lady Longworth's thin hand fidgeted on the table. "More so than you, it would seem."

"I beg your pardon?"

"You didn't waste any time before asking her to marry you."

"No, because I didn't need any time," Nicholas replied simply. "I love Lavinia. I always have. And she loves me."

"Yes, even while she was married to that Frenchman!" His mother shook her head. "I've never heard of such behaviour. In my day, a woman stayed married to the same man her whole life."

For the first time that evening, Nicholas was actually tempted to laugh. "For heaven's sake, Mother, Lavinia didn't have any choice in the matter. Her husband was killed. No doubt she would have remained married to him if he hadn't been."

His mother raked him over with her piercing gaze. "Yes, and all that time lusting after you."

"Lusting!" Nicholas hastily put down his glass. "Lavinia is not the type of woman to go *lusting* after any man. She has always conducted herself with the utmost propriety, and even you cannot deny that she has an excellent standing within the ton. There is not a hostess in London who would turn her away. Even Countess Lieven holds her in high regard, and she is not a lady easily pleased."

"Humph," Lady Longworth said again. "And I suppose you would have wasted your life waiting for her even if her husband had not died so conveniently."

Longworth ran his finger along the stem of the wineglass, a nerve jumping in his cheek. "I have been in love with Lavinia since first meeting her, that much I admit. But it was hardly my fault that I met her on the day she was being married to another man!"

"A lot of time has passed since then, Nicholas," his mother pointed out.

"Yes. And in all that time, I have not met anyone to compare with her."

"Fiddlesticks! You haven't even tried," Lady Longworth replied mumpishly. "You've spent more time at your sports, and in the company of Lord Marwood and his friends, than you have in the company of ladies. You could have had your pick of any number of suitable, well-connected young misses, Nicholas. Instead, you chose to waste your time pining over a married woman. A married woman!" she repeated, her voice rising in agitation. "How do you think that made me feel?"

"I shouldn't have thought it would have made you feel one way or another." Longworth's voice was deceptively quiet. "My name has never been linked with Lavinia's, nor have I ever given you the least cause for embarrassment as a result of my involvement with her. I have always observed propriety. I should have thought you would have been relieved that I was not given to the foolish, headstrong impulses of many of my friends."

"I understand that, Nicholas, but—"

"Instead, you tell me to start acting like a soon-to-be married man and to be mindful of my obligations." Nicholas rose and stood staring down at her almost sadly. "Well, let me tell you, Mother, I am very well aware of my responsibilities. I am not ashamed of anything I have ever done in my life, nor do I intend to start making any changes now. I love Lavinia Duplesse, and I intend to marry her. And I will not hear another word spoken against her, by you or anyone else!''

His mother's cheeks flushed painfully. ''Nicholas, you don't understand—''

''On the contrary, Mother, I understand perfectly. I understand that you have taken it into your head not to accept Lavinia, and that you've not even had the decency to invite her here. Very well, that is your choice. But like it or not, Lavinia is going to be the next viscountess and nothing you can say will change that. And as for my going away now, I have given my word to someone and I intend to keep it. Yes, I realize that I am soon to be married, and while I do not expect you to understand my reasons for going, you might at least try to show some confidence in my ability to make an intelligent decision. Good evening, Mother.''

With that, Nicholas turned on his heel and marched from the room. The door closed with a firm click behind him.

In the silence following his departure, Lady Longworth stared into the flickering candlelight, her eyes filling with tears as she recalled the anger in her son's voice.

Oh, Nicholas. How could you think I had no confidence in you? She was more proud of her only son than she had ever been of anyone in her life. She had watched him grow from a round-cheeked baby into a man to be proud of. She had followed his progress through Oxford with shining eyes, proud of the fact that, unlike so many of her friends' sons, Nicholas had never been sent down. She had watched him graduate from university, and then go on to the military. The Horse Guards, no less, Lady Longworth thought, her heart swelling with pride.

And then she had watched him fall in love.

Lady Longworth bit her lip and lifted her eyes upwards, trying to hold back the tears that trembled on her lashes. Oh, yes, she had known the day it had happened. Nicholas had gone to the Honourable Lavinia Ridgley's wedding to the much older and already widowed François Duplesse and had come home afterwards with the strangest glow in his eyes.

Like any mother, she had hoped that the romantic mood of the wedding had rubbed off on him, or that he had perhaps met someone there. But when, in the days following the wedding, Nicholas had not called upon any of the eligible young ladies he had seen, nor mentioned anyone's name, Lady Longworth had begun to realize why. Her son had fallen in love with the very woman whose marriage he had gone to celebrate. And he had remained true to her ever since.

Lady Longworth pulled her shawl more closely

around her thin shoulders as Mortimer made his way silently back into the room.

"Will that be all, my lady?"

Lady Longworth nodded wearily. "Yes, thank you, Mortimer. I think I shall retire for the night."

She turned towards the door, her mind going back to her conversation with Nicholas. It was true enough, what he had said. He had never once disgraced himself, or her. Whatever amorous liaisons he may have enjoyed were conducted with dignity and the utmost discretion. Never once had the ugly taint of scandal touched his head.

And now that Lavinia Duplesse was widowed, he was free to marry the only woman he had ever loved, taking him that last, irrevocable step away from Lady Longworth and out of her life. And instead of congratulating him, all she had been able to do was berate and badger him. Was it any wonder he had turned away from her in anger? If only she had the chance to take back what she had said, the viscountess thought sadly, one tear making its way slowly down her lined cheek.

CHAPTER TWO

WEARING THE MAGNIFICENT sapphire gown, Lavinia slowly descended the stairs, very conscious of Nicholas's gaze upon her. She saw the warm glow of admiration in his eyes and felt a tingle of excitement as he reached out his hand and enfolded her fingers in his own.

The gown was indeed a credit to the dressmaker's skill. Shimmering with a life of its own, the richly coloured satin accentuated the whiteness of Lavinia's skin. Her neck and smooth, creamy shoulders were bare, the moderately shallow *décolletage* of the gown just displaying the soft fullness of the tops of her breasts.

Her maid, Hélène, had done an artful job of arranging her long, luxuriant tresses in an elaborate coiffure, winding a ribbon of sapphire velvet, studded with diamonds, throughout. Around her throat, Lavinia wore Nicholas's engagement present to her, a stunning circle of brilliant white diamonds set with sapphires. Matching earrings dangled from her earlobes, while completing the set, a beautiful diamond-and-sapphire engagement ring twinkled on her finger.

Nicholas had not asked his mother for the Longworth diamonds. Even though they were rightfully his, he had known that she would have balked at giving them to him because of Lavinia. Instead, he had gone to Rundel and Bridge and commissioned a new set of jewellery for his future wife. Better that Lavinia never see the Longworth diamonds at all than be forced to wear them unhappily.

But now, as he gazed up at her, Nicholas could not have been more pleased.

"You look magnificent. Everything about you is breathtaking."

Lavinia coloured prettily, but did not look away. "I am so glad you approve."

"Did you choose the dress to go with the jewels, or the other way round?"

Lavinia's laugh was light and charming. "I admit, it was not my original intention, but once I saw the material, I realized it would make a stunning backdrop for them."

Nicholas joined in her laughter, marvelling that he was actually to marry this incredible creature. "No, it is you who provide the backdrop, my love," he whispered, lightly touching the stones. "These are mere decorations."

Nicholas bent his head, brushing his mouth

gently across hers. The scent of her cologne mingling with the provocative fragrance of her own body intoxicated him. He dropped his mouth lower to kiss the pulse point in her throat, feeling the icy coldness of the diamonds against the heat of her skin—a heady combination.

"Nicholas!"

His name was a throaty whisper on her lips as she clung to him. She had waited so very long to be with him. Through all the long nights of her marriage to François, Lavinia had dreamt of him, longed for him. When François had made love to her, she had seen Nicholas's face, imagined it was Nicholas's body merging with her own. And now soon, so very soon, there would be no more need for pretending....

"Maman?" a voice said tentatively.

At the sound of her stepdaughter's voice, Lavinia felt the colour deepen in her cheeks and abruptly brought her errant thoughts back to the present. She stepped out of her fiancé's arms and turned to see Martine standing uncertainly on the top step, her cheeks flushed the same delicate pink as her gown. "I am sorry, I did not mean to disturb you—"

"It's all right, Martine, you did not disturb us. Come and say hello to Nicholas," Lavinia said softly.

Nicholas watched the young girl descend the staircase, marvelling, as always, that this charming *ingénue* could be François Duplesse's daughter. She must have taken after her mother, Nicholas decided. There was no physical resemblance to her father at all, and there were certainly no shared personality traits. While Nicholas had had the utmost respect for the Frenchman's abilities, he had never warmed to François as a friend.

"Good evening, Martine," Nicholas greeted her. "You look lovely tonight. Indeed, it will be an honour to be seen escorting the two most beautiful ladies here."

Martine smiled, the awkwardness of the moment gone. "*Merci*, Nicholas. Does *maman* not look beautiful?"

Nicholas turned back to his fiancée and slowly lifted her hand to his lips. "Indeed she does, Martine. Indeed she does."

Lavinia lifted her free hand to stroke his cheek, her eyes glowing. "Have you been to see your mother, Nicholas? Is she coming?"

"Actually, no." Nicholas cleared his throat awkwardly. "She has not been feeling too well of late. She...didn't think she would be quite up to it tonight."

Lavinia watched Nicholas's eyes and listened to his words, well aware that they were not telling the same story. She managed a game smile. "I am so sorry to hear that she has not been well. Perhaps next time."

Nicholas nodded. "Yes. Perhaps."

Lavinia turned as her butler arrived. "Is everything ready, Habinger?"

"Yes, Lady Duplesse."

"Good. I should think our guests will begin arriving shortly."

The words had barely left her lips before there was a knock on the door. Quickly squeezing her hand for luck, Longworth took his place next to her as Habinger went to open it.

Lavinia's face lit with pleasure as she recognized the first of their guests. "Edward! Laura! How wonderful to see you both."

Edward Kingsley stepped forward and kissed her warmly on the cheek. "Lavinia, my dear, you look absolutely radiant. And Nicholas." He turned to enclose his good friend's outstretched hand in a firm grip. "I vow you're looking quite the April gentleman. Or very nearly."

"Thank you, Edward. I must say, I never thought to see it happen," Nicholas admitted, recalling Lavinia's dangerous rescue from France. "And Miss Beaufort, what a pleasure to see you again."

Laura Beaufort was looking enchanting in a

gown of soft peach sarcenet. She had always been a pretty girl, but since the announcement of her own betrothal to Edward Kingsley, she had blossomed.

"Lord Longworth," Laura replied warmly, before reaching forward to press her cheek against Lavinia's. "Lavinia, you look absolutely wonderful tonight!"

"Thank you, Laura. I am so glad the two of you could come. May I present my stepdaughter, Martine."

Martine curtsied gracefully. "I am very pleased to meet you."

"But what a lovely gown, Miss Duplesse," Laura complimented her. "And such a pretty colour."

"It was a gift from *maman*," Martine told her. "The colour reminded me of the roses that grew wild in the fields around the château."

Laura's eyes warmed sympathetically. "Do you miss your home, Martine?"

"Sometimes," the girl admitted. "But I am very 'appy to be 'ere with *maman*," she said, her English slipping just a little. "This is my home now."

Nicholas turned back to Edward. "When are the newlyweds due back from Italy?"

Edward chuckled. "Who can say? I wasn't able to get a sensible word out of Charlotte once Devon arrived back in England.'' He leaned forward and lowered his voice in amusement. ''Love seems to make babbling fools of us all. But I'll say one thing, it certainly agrees with you, my friend.''

Nicholas nodded, his chest swelling with pride as he glanced at Lavinia, now chatting with Laura. ''I can hardly credit how happy I am, Edward. I never thought it would happen.'' His eyes darkened slightly at the thought of what lay ahead. ''But we must talk, my friend. There has been a development in France.''

Edward nodded briefly. ''Yes, so I understand.'' He purposely kept a smile on his face for the benefit of the ladies and the other guests who were arriving. ''At the club, later tonight?''

Nicholas nodded, and then rejoined Lavinia as Laura and Edward moved on into the reception room.

The next few hours flew by as Lavinia and Nicholas mingled with their guests, accepting the good wishes of close friends and distant acquaintances. It was a large group that had gathered to celebrate the engagement, although some of the guests had come more out of curiosity than from a desire to congratulate the couple.

It was well known that Lavinia's first husband, the Comte du Duplesse, had wasted no time in removing his young bride from England. Immediately after their marriage, he had ensconced her in his sprawling old château in the French countryside.

Lavinia had not returned to her native England once during her four years of marriage. And now that she was back, there were many who were anxious to see how, or if, she had changed.

Unfortunately, those who had come expecting to see a woman ill at ease in London Society were destined to be disappointed. Lavinia was as gracious, as elegant and as charming as anyone could have wished. She took time to speak to everyone in that uniquely soft, throaty voice of hers. And there was no doubting her devotion to her late husband's seventeen-year-old daughter.

In fact, it was the stepdaughter to whom some of the more marriage-minded mamas took exception. With that perfect skin and those huge, soulful eyes there was no denying that Martine Duplesse was a diamond. And with a sweetness of nature not unlike that of her youthful stepmother, she quickly won a place in many hearts, including those of a few of the young men present.

But it was Nicholas and Lavinia themselves who drew the bulk of the comments and stares that night. That they were totally in love was so obvious that it actually brought a tear to the eyes of a few hardened tabbies. The newly engaged pair had but to glance across the room at each other, their eyes locking in silent communication, to show how deeply committed they were.

At midnight, Edward called for everyone's attention.

"Ladies and gentlemen, a moment if you please." He waited for the chatter to die down before continuing. "Now, we all know why we are here. My good friend Nicholas has finally had the good sense to propose to one of the loveliest ladies in London, and Lavinia, poor creature, was foolish enough to accept. No, seriously now," Edward amended, laughing as the expected jeers and protests greeted his remark, "we are here to celebrate the forthcoming marriage of these two splendid people, and to that end, I would ask all of you to raise your glasses and join me in a toast to them. May they know only happiness and joy in their lives together." Edward raised his glass and smiled at them both. "To Nicholas and Lavinia."

"Nicholas and Lavinia!" the crowd echoed.

In the centre of the room, Nicholas waited until silence resumed before raising his own glass to the woman standing beside him. "To you, my darling Lavinia," he said in a strong, clear voice. "for making me the happiest man alive, and for bringing joy into my life after so many years of loneliness. I can never thank you enough. I can only say that I love you, and that I will always love you.''

Lavinia blinked rapidly and raised her own glass. ''And I love you, Nicholas. So very, very much.''

And then, to everyone's delight, Nicholas leaned forward and placed a long, lingering kiss on Lavinia's lips. Ignoring the cheers and laughter that resulted, he pulled her lovingly into his arms. And when he reluctantly drew back, it was to see the shimmer of tears in her eyes.

''Oh, Nicholas,'' she whispered tremulously.

''To Lavinia,'' Nicholas said, his eyes holding hers as he raised his glass.

''To Lavinia!'' shouted the now equally emotional crowd.

Amidst a great deal of eye wiping and throat clearing, the festivities carried on. Finally, at half past one, the last of the guests departed, leaving only Edward and Laura standing in the quiet of the hall with their hosts.

Nicholas sighed his satisfaction. ''Well, I would say that was an unmitigated success.'' He put his arm around Lavinia's waist and gave it a gentle squeeze. ''Everyone here tonight was captivated by you, my darling.''

Lavinia laughed. ''Impossible creature,'' she

whispered fondly. "It was you they were charmed by."

Across from her, Laura couldn't help but smile. "Do you know, I actually saw Lady Harrington wipe a tear from her eye when you made that toast to Lavinia, Nicholas. I don't think I have ever seen her so moved."

Nicholas shrugged. "I only spoke the truth."

"Ah, but that's the thing," Edward said, grinning. "The members of the ton aren't used to hearing the truth, especially when it comes to sentiments of the heart."

"I think what the English are not used to is two people who are truly in love," Martine said suddenly.

Lavinia turned to look at her stepdaughter in surprise. "What do you mean, Martine?"

"Well, you and Nicholas are so obviously devoted to each other, and you are not ashamed to show it. It happens seldom, *n'est-ce pas?* Are not most aristocratic marriages made for convenience?"

"Yes, a lot of them are," Nicholas granted, "but I am happy to say that I know of at least two marriages besides ours that are not. What say you, Kingsley?"

Edward drew a similarly blushing Laura into his

embrace. "I am the first to agree, and I know I speak for my sister as well."

Lavinia stepped forward to put an arm around Martine's shoulders. "Off you go to bed, Martine. It has been a big night for you."

Martine guiltily stifled a yawn. "*Oui,* I am tired," she admitted. *"Bonsoir."*

"Good night, Martine," Nicholas said fondly.

The others said their good-nights and watched the girl climb the stairs. When she had gone, Laura said, "Lavinia, your stepdaughter is charming."

"Yes, I daresay she will be in great demand," Edward put in, adding with a smile, "I saw Lord Hardy's son desperately trying to get her attention earlier."

"Yes, but I think she preferred the company of young Tomkins," Nicholas said. "Although she did spend a fair bit of time talking to Sir Wilber's boy."

Lavinia sighed. "The problem with Martine is that all of this is so new to her. François kept her very sheltered, and I truly don't think she realizes how attractive she is. I had to reprimand her earlier for allowing Lord Fox to take her out onto the terrace—alone."

"I'm sure you needn't worry, Lavinia," Laura reassured her. "She will quickly come to learn what is and is not acceptable behaviour."

"I do hope so," Lavinia murmured. "She is so very trusting of people right now. I should hate to see her get hurt."

"She won't," Nicholas asserted. "Not if I have anything to say about it."

"I say, Nicholas, what happens with regard to Martine?" Edward enquired. "Does she legally become your stepdaughter?"

Nicholas glanced at Lavinia, his expression questioning. "I'd really never thought about that. Does she?"

"I suppose so. She is legally *my* stepdaughter." Lavinia's lips quirked. "And do not a wife's possessions become her husband's once they marry?"

"What a splendid arrangement," Edward quipped. "A wife and a fully grown daughter into the bargain."

"A fully grown one, until we have one of our own," Nicholas corrected him.

"Nicholas!"

Nicholas turned, and was amused to see the colour in Lavinia's face. "Now, darling, don't scold," he said gently. "Children are a natural result of being in love. Isn't that right, Edward?"

"As I recall."

"In fact," Nicholas continued, "given the relative closeness of our weddings, I think it will be interesting to see which couple publishes a birth announcement first.''

"Don't forget Charlotte," Edward reminded him. "She and Marwood have a bit of a head start on the rest of us."

"Edward, really!" Laura said, colouring hotly. "This is hardly suitable conversation for mixed company. I shall tell your sister when she returns that you were discussing her so indelicately."

"Do that, my sweet," Edward said wickedly, "and I guarantee that if Charlotte is not already in the family way, she will dutifully cast me off for having accused her of being so!"

To the sound of laughter and good-natured teasing, Laura and Edward left, finally leaving Nicholas and Lavinia alone. Returning to the elegant drawing-room, Nicholas pulled Lavinia into his arms and tilted her face up to his.

Their lips came together in a kiss of mutual need and longing. He felt the softness of her body melt against the hard length of his as his hands curved into the small of her back. He heard her breath catch as his lips moved round to nuzzle the tender skin beneath her earlobe.

"God, you're beautiful!" he murmured, following the line of her neck and bare shoulder. He felt her shiver as his lips reverently brushed the top of her breasts.

Lavinia moaned low in her throat. "Nicholas, you must...stop."

"I don't want to stop." His mouth came back to hers, catching her lips still parted on a sigh. Her breath was sweet and warm, and he groaned, feeling his desire intensify. "I want you so much."

"And I want you, but I hardly think this is the time or the place," Lavinia replied unsteadily. Her eyes twinkled. "Martine has never been a deep sleeper."

The warning in her voice cut through Nicholas's passion, and he reluctantly set her away from him, knowing that the longer he held her, the harder it would be to leave. "My sweet Lavinia," he said with a chuckle, "am I ever to see you lose your self-control altogether and throw yourself impetuously into my arms?"

"Oh, indeed, my lord. And before too much longer, I shouldn't wonder. Especially if you carry on like that," she scolded.

"Yes, well, I can only hope." Nicholas gazed down into her beautiful, trusting face, and his expression suddenly grew serious. He had to tell her that he was going away. It was only fair that she be prepared for his leaving within the next two days.

"Yes, Nicholas?" Lavinia said gently.

He heard the concern in her voice and took a

deep breath. "Lavinia, there's...something I have to tell—"

He broke off as the door to the salon unexpectedly opened to reveal Habinger standing in the doorway.

"Oh, forgive me, my lady," the flustered butler said. "It was just that, well, it was so quiet in here, I thought everyone had...left."

The butler's arrival shattered the mood of intimacy and caused Nicholas to abruptly change his mind. No, he wouldn't tell her tonight. He couldn't spoil what had been such a special evening for both of them. Let Lavinia have her dreams tonight. There would be time enough for worry tomorrow.

"That's quite all right, Habinger, I was just leaving."

Lavinia touched Nicholas's sleeve with her hand. "Nicholas? I thought you were about to tell me—"

"What I was going to say can wait, my darling," Nicholas assured her. "Right now, I think I'd best leave or the servants will be up all night." He drew her into his arms and pressed a tender kiss against her temple. "Sleep well."

"Shall I see you tomorrow?"

Nicholas nodded. "Yes. I'll come by in the

morning.'' He tried to meet her eyes, but couldn't. He knew he would have no choice but to tell her then.

NICHOLAS LEFT LAVINIA'S house that night, understanding for the first time the kind of anguish his good friend Lord Marwood had experienced the night he had taken leave of the woman he loved before sailing for France to undertake a dangerous mission—the very mission that had brought Lavinia safely home to England. Now Nicholas knew what it was like to face the prospect of never seeing one's beloved again.

Directing his driver to take him to White's, Nicholas climbed into the carriage. A short while later, he found himself in the comfortably masculine ambience of the gentlemen's club's darkly panelled interior. Edward was waiting for him at a quiet table in the back corner, where they could talk without fear of being overheard.

''I've ordered brandy for both of us,'' Edward said as Nicholas sat down. ''I thought you might be able to use one.''

''Yes, I've a feeling I will.'' Nicholas gave him a lopsided grin. ''And probably a few more before I see Lavinia again tomorrow.''

''You haven't told her then?''

He shook his head. ''I was going to tell her tonight, but I changed my mind. I didn't want to spoil such a pleasant evening.''

''So tell me, how did this all come about?'' Edward enquired. He glanced around carefully and then leaned closer. ''Osborne told me he wasn't willing to risk either of us going back to France to find Leclerc.''

''That's what he told me, too, but when I saw the names of the chaps he was contemplating sending, I told him it would be like sending lambs to the slaughter.''

''That bad?'' Edward grimaced. ''So how did you convince him?''

''By telling him that the only way Leclerc was likely to come out of hiding was by sending to France someone he wanted badly enough that he'd risk showing himself. I also told Osborne that if Leclerc wasn't stopped *before* he got to England, it would be a damned sight more difficult to stop him after.''

They broke off momentarily as the waiter arrived with their brandy. Setting the tray with a bottle and two glasses on the small table beside Edward, the man moved off, leaving Nicholas to continue, ''Osborne isn't positive that the drawing Baker sent is of Leclerc, and with us not being able to positively identify the man, the chances of nabbing him once he's in England are limited indeed.

That's why I stressed the importance of flushing him out in his own territory."

While Nicholas was speaking, Edward poured out two glasses of cognac and handed one to his friend. "That's all well and good, but what if you meet the same fate as all the others? Leclerc is no novice at this game. He's damn good. The fact that no one has been able to get to him proves that."

"Yes, but it's his cockiness I'm counting on to trip him up," Nicholas admitted. "Given his rather formidable list of successes in the past, I doubt he will view the arrival of yet another English agent, even one of my reputation, as a particularly imposing threat. And knowing how close he is to leaving France, I am hoping he may grow a little careless."

"Well, I have to say I don't envy you having to tell Lavinia you're going back to France. I remember how she looked when Marwood brought her back. She was scared to death."

"Yes, I know," Nicholas said ruefully. "She's already admitted to me that she never expected to get out of France alive." He breathed a heavy sigh. "And now I have to tell her that I'm going back in."

"Do you think telling her that you're trying to find the man who was responsible for her husband's death will help?"

"Not in the least. In fact, I don't intend to tell Lavinia why I'm going."

"You're not?"

Nicholas shook his head. "Lavinia has obviously heard of Jean Leclerc, and she may or may not suspect that he is the one behind her husband's death. If I tell her that I am going to France to try to find Leclerc, she'll worry herself sick."

"Then how do you intend to broach the subject?" Edward asked.

"I don't know. I'm almost tempted to say I'm just going up to the north of England for a few days. Or down to the coast. Lord knows, it really doesn't make much difference."

Edward drew a deep breath and gazed into the depths of the amber liquid in his glass. "I for one shall be heartily glad when this damned war is over."

"Yes, so shall I, my friend. But the problem with men like Leclerc is that it's never really over," Nicholas said grimly. "For them, the killing goes on. That's why I have to stop him before he gets to England. We can't afford to have Leclerc slip into London Society and then start doing away with whomsoever he pleases." He glanced at Edward sharply. "I'm afraid none of us would be able to rest safely in our beds if that were to happen."

"LORD LONGWORTH, my lady."

"Thank you, Habinger." Lavinia rose and went to greet her fiancé at the door. "Good morning, my lord. I had not thought to see you here quite so early."

"Good morning." Nicholas drew her into his arms and kissed her long and tenderly. "You are looking exceptionally lovely this morning."

"I should be." Lavinia flashed a grin at him. "I am expecting a handsome gentleman caller. Dear me, I do hope he doesn't arrive while you're here."

Nicholas's lips curved in a devilish smile. "Saucy wench, tease me, will you?" He playfully tapped her behind as she went to sit down.

"Nicholas! Behave!"

"I will, but only for the moment. Is Martine up?"

Lavinia shook her head fondly. "Not yet. I fear last night quite tired her out. She hasn't grown accustomed to these late nights yet." She gazed at Nicholas through eyes made perceptive by love. "You look weary, though. Did you not go directly home after you left here?"

"Not immediately, no." Nicholas knew he could not lie to her. "I met Edward at the club and we chatted for a while."

Lavinia frowned, detecting a change in Nicholas

she wasn't quite able to identify. "Is everything all right, Nicholas?"

He slowly sat down on the settee beside her. "Lavinia, there's something we have to discuss. Or rather, something I have to tell you."

"Yes, I gathered as much last night." Lavinia's smile faded. "Is this serious?"

"Yes."

"I knew it. What's wrong, Nicholas?"

"Well, there's nothing…wrong, exactly."

"Then what is it…exactly?"

"I'm…going back to France."

"What?"

He heard the horror and disbelief in her voice and forced himself to go on. "There is a matter that needs taking care of, and I…told Lord Osborne I would go."

Lavinia stared at him in shock. "But how can you even think of returning to France after what happened when you went to rescue Edward? The French will still be looking for you, Nicholas. You can't possibly go back there now!"

"Lavinia, no one is going to be looking for me," Nicholas said, trying his best to reassure her. "The war is almost over. Bonaparte's intelligence network is all but dispersed."

"Then why are you going at all?" Lavinia enquired sharply. "Did Lord Osborne ask you to?"

"No, not exactly," Nicholas replied. "But the mission is…delicate enough to require the services of a more…seasoned agent."

"A more seasoned agent." Lavinia rose to her feet, the rapid rise and fall of her chest evidence that she was more than a little agitated. "Nicholas, I know it is not my place to tell you what you should and should not do, but in this instance, I beg you to reconsider. We are to be married in less than a month. What if—" she closed her eyes and turned her back towards him "—what if something were to…happen to you?"

Nicholas rose and went to stand behind her. "Nothing is going to happen, my love. I shall go, I shall take care of this business and then I shall return. Simple."

"If it is so simple, why are you not willing to let one of Osborne's other men go?" Lavinia rounded on him. "Why does this mission require the services of a *seasoned agent?*"

Nicholas tried to affect an air of nonchalance. "Lavinia, you're making far too much of this."

"Am I? I don't think so." Lavinia stared into his eyes, searching for the truth. "You're not telling me everything, Nicholas. I know you better than that. Why are you going to France? Why is this mission so important?"

Nicholas managed a convincing smile. "Every

mission is important, Lavinia. No one knows that better than you. You were intimately involved from the moment you married François.''

"Then tell me what this is about.''

He shook his head sadly. "I cannot.''

"Can't or won't?'' Lavinia held her breath. There was so much he wasn't telling her and she was horribly afraid. Afraid that she was going to lose him just when their life together was about to begin.

"Nicholas, *please* let someone else go. Please do not put me through this torture. I cannot bear the thought of losing you.''

Nicholas sighed and pulled her into the circle of his arms, willing her to draw strength and confidence from his embrace. "I can't, Lavinia. If it were less important, I would gladly step aside and let another man take my place. But the consequences of this mission not being successfully carried out are too dangerous to contemplate. I know I can do what has to be done.''

Lavinia stepped back out of his arms, afraid that she would burst into tears if she stayed there. The ache in her heart made her want to get down on her knees and beg him not to go. What would she do if he didn't come back? How could she face the rest of her life if Nicholas were killed?

Watching her, Nicholas felt her withdrawal like

a physical pain. "Lavinia, please do not distance yourself from me," he pleaded. "I need you now more than ever. I need your strength."

"I have no strength, Nicholas," she told him sadly. "Not for this. I cannot help but remember what it was like when Lord Marwood came to take me out of France. It was so dangerous...." Her words trailed off as memories too painful to remember crept in to choke her.

Suddenly, she looked up at him. "My God, that's it, isn't it? You are going in order to find someone."

Inwardly, Nicholas flinched. The workings of Lavinia's agile mind constantly surprised him. "I am going to look for someone, yes."

"And when you find him?" Her eyes cleared for a moment. "Is this another rescue mission?"

He knew that she was grasping at straws, and he was almost tempted to lie and let her believe it. But he knew he couldn't. It wouldn't be fair. "No, I am not going to...rescue anyone, my love."

A tense silence developed between them. "Then you are going to kill someone," Lavinia said in a flat, dead voice. Dear God, he was putting himself in such danger. "Nicholas, please, I *beg* you to reconsider."

It was only because Nicholas knew Lavinia's own life was in danger that he didn't change his mind and back out of the mission then and there. Her name was on Leclerc's list, too. If he did not go, and the man who was sent to kill Leclerc failed, the danger to everyone would be that much greater. Better to chance his own life than to put the lives of others at risk. Especially Lavinia's.

"I cannot. There is…too much at stake," he said, inadvertently quoting Osborne's words.

Lavinia walked slowly towards the window, focusing her attention on anything she could to distract her mind from the fact that he was leaving. He saw the fear in her eyes when she turned to face him, as well as the weary resignation. "Nicholas, *please*."

"I will come back, Lavinia," Nicholas told her urgently. "I promise I will return, and then we'll be married, just as we had planned. Nothing will stop me from having you now, beloved. Nothing!"

CHAPTER THREE

Two DAYS LATER, Nicholas made his way along a darkened country road, heading towards the small village of Rosières just southeast of Amien. Through contacts, he had learned that a man matching Leclerc's description had recently been seen at Le Cheval Blanc, a small country inn near Rosières. That, at least, had been good news. It meant that Leclerc's business in France was not yet concluded.

Arriving at the inn just before eight o'clock in the evening, Nicholas left his horse with the young boy at the stable. Then, pulling his hood up over his head, he made his way towards the bustling *auberge*. Nicholas knew the dangers inherent with his being in France, even though he had assured Osborne there were none. For that reason, he had dressed in the clothes of a simple cleric, a disguise he had used on more than one occasion, and with considerable success. He pulled out his missal and tucked it under his arm.

The sounds of revelry and laughter hit him as

soon he opened the heavy wooden door. Nicholas glanced around the crowded room, noting the faces of the people gathered about the tables. He took care not to stare at any one person too long. He had no wish to arouse curiosity, nor to draw attention to himself. Adopting the humble manner of a priest, he approached the innkeeper. *"Monsieur?"*

The innkeeper, a large, heavy-set man with dark, beady eyes, and a bulbous nose dominating his meaty features, turned and barked, *"Oui?"* Then, seeing the clerical garb, he added more politely, in rapid French, "Excuse me, Father. What can I get for you?"

Nicholas smiled benevolently. "Only a room for the night, my son," he replied, in equally fluent French.

Fortunately, the innkeeper had one room left. It was small and noisy, being located at the top of the stairs. But it was not as bad as some, and as he had no intention of sleeping, Nicholas gratefully took it. If Leclerc was still in the area, he would likely return to the inn for the night. If not, there was always the possibility that Nicholas might overhear something of use from one of the revellers.

Once in the room, Nicholas took off his serviceable brown cloak and laid it on the bed, revealing the cleric's tunic beneath. He then crossed to the window and looked out onto the courtyard below, silently blessing his good fortune. From his window, he had a clear view of the yard.

He carefully pulled the curtain aside an inch or so, and stood watching the people coming and going—until an unexpected knock on his bedroom door caused him to drop the curtain and step away from the window. He tensed, his hand dropping automatically to the butt of his pistol. *"Oui?"*

It was only a serving girl with the simple dinner he had requested. Nicholas let out a breath. He was getting jumpy. Still, the crusty bread and thick slices of cheese felt good in his stomach. He had not stopped for food anywhere along the road, and it had been a long time since breakfast. He tucked one piece of bread into the pocket of his gown for the long night ahead. Then he took up his watch by the window again.

An hour passed. Two. The sounds from the ale-room downstairs grew louder as the locals imbibed more heavily. Nicholas purposely kept the room in darkness, ensuring that he would not be seen from the road. He tensed briefly when a large, burly man suddenly staggered drunkenly out through the front doors of the inn and collapsed in a heap on the ground. But it was obviously nothing. Moments later, a number of his friends came out, picked him up and dragged him back inside.

Close to midnight, Nicholas heard the sound of footsteps in the hall outside his doorway. Leaving the window for a moment, he tiptoed across the room and put his ear to the door. The sound of feminine laughter, as well as a few unmistakable French phrases spoken in a rough masculine voice set his mind at rest. Obviously, the ladies of the evening were beginning to retire. Another high-pitched laugh and the sound of a door slamming next to his own room confirmed it.

Well, at least there was pleasure for some, Nicholas reflected drily, trying to ignore the sounds coming through the thin walls of the room next door. He returned to his place by the window. And not a moment too soon. A closed carriage drawn by a matched pair of greys had pulled into the courtyard.

Nicholas carefully drew back into the shadows. As he watched, the coachman sprang down from the box, and after glancing around the deserted yard, made directly for the inn. Moments later he returned with the innkeeper. He then rapped sharply on the door of the carriage.

Nicholas held his breath as the door opened and a man stepped down. Could this be Leclerc?

It was difficult to tell. The man's curly brimmed beaver hat was pulled down low over his eyes, while the turned-up collar of the multicaped greatcoat made it almost impossible to see his features. But there was no mistaking the furtiveness of his movements, alerting Nicholas to the presence of danger.

The three men spoke in low, urgent whispers. An argument seemed to be ensuing between the innkeeper and the coachman. The innkeeper kept shaking his head and pointing to the road, while the coachman stamped his foot and pointed at the inn. Nicholas tried to get a better look at the face of the passenger, but he stubbornly kept his head down.

"Come along, *mon ami,* let's have a look at your face," Nicholas whispered softly. "Look up, damn it!"

Strangely enough, as if hearing his appeal, Fate chose that moment to intervene. The couple in the next room suddenly brought their lovemaking to a dramatic conclusion. Nicholas heard the high keening sound of the woman's voice raised in pleasure, and then a resounding crash—clearly of the bed collapsing—as the man grunted and reached his own shuddering pinnacle.

The three men in the yard glanced upwards, the sound having drawn their attention. Nicholas saw the man he suspected of being Leclerc reach instinctively under his cape. For a split second he looked up, his eyes scanning the windows on the second floor.

It was all the time Nicholas needed. There was no mistaking that face. It was the same as the one in the picture on Osborne's desk. He had found Jean Leclerc!

Nicholas watched as the innkeeper put his hand on Leclerc's arm and murmured something unintelligible. Leclerc's hand slowly slid out from under his cape and then he chuckled, obviously recognizing what had happened. After glancing around, the three men resumed their conversation.

Nicholas moved closer to the window again, straining to hear what they were saying. The voices were low, as though the men were fearful of being overheard. Only one word came clearly to his ears before Leclerc climbed back into the landau and the carriage set off—*Calais!*

So it was true, Nicholas admitted grimly. Leclerc was planning to make for the coast. No doubt a ship waited even now to convey him across the Channel. He would be in England by morning. There was absolutely no time to waste. Nicholas had to stop Leclerc before he reached the coast!

He reached for his cloak. Reversing it this time so that the black side was turned out, he gathered up his few belongings and left the room. Every minute counted now. He had to cut off Leclerc's escape before it was too late.

Avoiding the busy front entrance of the inn, Nicholas located the back stairs and silently made his way down. He sprinted across the yard to the darkened stables. The horses nickered nervously at his approach. He crept stealthily between the stalls, looking for his mount. Suddenly, he froze, detecting a movement against some bales of hay at the back. He reached for his pistol and drew back into a stall. "Show yourself!" he growled, forgetting for a moment to speak in French.

Nicholas heard a startled gasp. "Do not shoot, *monsieur,* do not shoot!" a young and very frightened voice whispered back in French.

The sinister presence turned out to be nothing more than the young lad who had stabled his horse, and Nicholas quickly put his pistol away. He stepped out of the stall, a dark, shadowy figure in his long, flowing black cape. "Do not be afraid, my child. It is only I," he said, this time in perfect French.

"Mon père?" The young boy's eyes widened until they almost filled his face. "What are you doing out here so late?"

Nicholas held his finger to his lips. "Silence, my son. Where is my horse?"

The boy swallowed and, in answer to the ques-

tion, ran down to the second stall. He quickly untied the chestnut and brought him out.

''Thank you.'' Nicholas sprang into the saddle
with far more agility than a travelling cleric would
ever have possessed, and tossed the lad a coin.
''God go with you, my son.'' Then, wheeling the
chestnut's head around, Nicholas set off in pursuit
of the carriage. He wished, not for the first time,
that he had his own fiery stallion under him, and
prayed that he hadn't heard the name of Leclerc's
intended destination wrong.

THE CARRIAGE HAD a good head start, but Nicholas
was able to catch up quickly. Unaware that he was
being pursued, the coachman did not set a break-
neck speed. Nicholas followed the road until he
heard the rumble of carriage wheels on the road
ahead. Rounding a bend, he spotted the vehicle
about a quarter of a mile ahead. At that point, he
guided his horse into the woods, knowing that the
trees would give him the necessary cover.

Nicholas quickly closed the distance, his mind
racing as fast as the horse's hooves. There was one
man inside the carriage, and the coachman on the
box. Nicholas had hoped to get Leclerc alone without shedding any other blood, but faced with the
prospect that both men would be armed, Nicholas
knew the possibility of that was slim. He didn't

want to waste a shot. He would bide his time, waiting for the man who had cold-bloodedly murdered his fiancé's husband.

Nicholas took stock of the countryside as, still hidden behind the line of trees, he drew level with the coach. They were approaching a long, deserted stretch of road. There were no houses in the area, although Nicholas saw what looked to be the dark outline of a barn and some scattered farm buildings set well back from the road. Fortunately, at this time of night, the occupants—likely hard-working farmers—would all be sound asleep. With any luck, the sound of gunfire would not waken them.

Nicholas's thoughts turned suddenly to Lavinia, and he knew a heart-wrenching moment of guilt. *Dear God, please let her forgive me if I do not return this night. I love you, my darling.* Then, putting aside all other considerations, Nicholas pulled out his pistol, took aim and fired.

The sound tore through the night like an explosion. As the coachman grabbed his shoulder and slumped forward, the horses whinnied in fear, their ears flat against their heads, their eyes rolling. Nicholas glimpsed the startled face of a man at the window and heard a voice shouting, "*Les chevaux!* Stop them!"

Yanking valiantly on the reins, the coachman managed to draw the panicked team to a halt before slipping from his seat unconscious, a dark stain spreading around the torn fabric at his shoulder. Nicholas stayed under cover of the trees, watching. There was no sound now but the nervous stamping of the horses. He saw no more faces at the window. Most likely Leclerc was on the floor, or sitting far enough back not to be hit by a stray bullet.

"Leclerc!" Nicholas shouted, his voice carrying clearly in the still night air. "Show yourself!"

There was no sound or movement from within the carriage.

"Leclerc! Come out and throw down your weapons."

"Who are you?" said a voice in heavily accented French.

"That is no concern of yours."

"On the contrary, it is of great concern. Why should I show myself to someone who would kill me?"

"How do you know that is my intention?" Nicholas replied.

"Because you are no highwayman," replied a second voice.

Nicholas raised an eyebrow in astonishment. *English?* His eyes narrowed. He had not expected Leclerc to have a travelling companion. And certainly not an English one.

"Come forward, Leclerc," he ordered. "You *and* your friend. I would have you both face me."

"Are you such a coward that you cannot also show yourself?" the Frenchman taunted. "Or do you intend to stay shut away in the woods like a cowering beast?"

Nicholas felt a hard knot of anger form within his breast. "Do you think me such a fool that I would set myself up as a target? Come out, gentlemen, and throw down your weapons." He waited a moment longer. "You gain nothing by remaining within, for I have the advantage. Your coachman will be taking you no further tonight. Come out, I say!"

Slowly the door opened. The two men stepped down. Nicholas immediately recognized the shorter one as the man he had seen at the inn. But when he glanced at the other man, he was astonished to see that the man's face was bandaged to the point of being unrecognizable. His arm also looked to be caught up in some kind of a sling.

"Come along, gentlemen, let's have your weapons. Slowly now," Nicholas cautioned them. "Don't try anything foolish."

He kept his pistol raised as they both reached under their coats. When he saw the two pistols hit the ground, he gently pressed his heels into the chestnut's sides. Emerging from cover for the first time, he approached them slowly, watching their faces. "So, we meet at last, *monsieur*," Nicholas said softly to Leclerc.

The Frenchman's eyes narrowed. "You know me?"

"I should. Your reputation precedes you."

Leclerc bowed mockingly. "I am flattered."

"You needn't be," Nicholas drawled. "It is not a reputation to be proud of."

He saw a momentary flash of anger in the man's dark eyes. "You should be careful, *monsieur*. I have many friends in France."

"Perhaps, but they do not concern me." Nicholas glanced at the other man. "Who is your wounded companion, Leclerc?"

"He is of no concern to you."

"On the contrary, anyone connected with you is of interest to me. And the fact that he is English makes him even more so." Nicholas addressed the man directly. "Who are you, sir, and where did you sustain your injuries?"

The man started to speak, but Leclerc quickly held up his hand, silencing him. "I told you, *monsieur*, that is no concern of yours."

Nicholas sighed and cocked his pistol. The sound echoed in the darkness. "Who is he?"

Leclerc swallowed. "*Monsieur*, I—"

Suddenly, a second gunshot ripped through the

night air, shattering the silence. Nicholas watched in disbelief as the Englishman behind Leclerc grabbed at the front of his coat and then crumpled lifeless to the ground.

Nicholas blanched. "What in blazes...?" He spun in the direction from which the shot had come, his pistol raised. Suddenly, out of the corner of his eye, he saw Leclerc pull a small, deadly looking pistol from his breast pocket and aim it directly at his chest.

Displaying the lightning-fast reflexes that had saved his life on more than one occasion, Nicholas whipped back round and flexed his finger on the trigger. There was the sound of a shot, and Leclerc staggered back against the carriage, grasping his chest. His own pistol discharged uselessly into the air.

Nicholas's face darkened. "It is over, Leclerc. There will be no more murders."

The dying man's eyes were glazed with fear, but he shook his head and laughed horribly. "*Non, mon ami,* it is...not over. You are...wrong." He laughed again, then slid to the road, uttering on his dying gasp, *"Je ne suis pas...Leclerc!"*

Nicholas stared at him in horror. Not Leclerc! Then who the hell—

A split second before the bullet hit, Nicholas heard the sound of a pistol cocking and instinctively dropped. But he wasn't fast enough. A fiery bolt tore into his flesh, knocking him out of the saddle. He hit the ground at the edge of the road, blood pouring from the wound in his side. Then he heard a very English, very cultured voice in the darkness above him.

"So, Longworth, you thought to prevent my leaving France, did you? Well, I'm afraid you thought wrong."

Nicholas gasped and closed his eyes as a fresh stab of pain hit him, causing his stomach to lurch violently. He felt the sweat trickling down his temple. He was going to be sick.

"Nothing to say, Nicholas?" the voice taunted him.

Nicholas fought to hold on to consciousness. Straining his eyes, he could just make out the figure of a tall man mounted upon a horse. He could not discern the man's features, but he could see a thin plume of smoke rising from the pistol in his hand.

"Who—who…?" Nicholas tried, but couldn't get the words out. He was becoming dizzy, growing steadily weaker from loss of blood. His body was on fire.

"Who am I? Is that what you're trying to say, old man?" The smooth English voice was mocking him. "But who do you think I am? I am the one you came to kill. I am Jean Leclerc."

Nicholas struggled to focus his eyes, aware of the chaotic jumble of thoughts spinning around in his brain.

They had the wrong man! The picture was of the wrong man!

"Yes, I've surprised you, haven't I, Nicholas? I must admit, I hadn't expected to. I thought for certain you would have seen through my little ruse."

"Ruse?" Nicholas wheezed out through pain-clenched teeth.

"Yes. The drawing I allowed Baker to have. Clever of me, don't you think? To have him send back a picture of the wrong man. Of course, he didn't suspect until it was too late," the man said smugly. "They never do. But I thought you might have. I know all about your reputation, you see. I could not believe you managed to sneak Kingsley out of France—and right under my nose, as it turns out. I suppose I should applaud your intelligence for that. But—" the man sighed dramatically "—I really had expected a more worthy opponent in a face-to-face confrontation."

"This was...hardly a...face-to-face...confrontation."

He heard the man chuckle. "Perhaps not. But at least it is not I who am lying in the ditch dying.

Tell me, Nicholas, is it more noble to die a hero or to live a coward? I wonder. I know which I should prefer.''

Nicholas licked his lips. Even the act of speaking was causing him excruciating pain. "So, it was all…a lie," he wheezed. "It was not…Leclerc."

"On the contrary, it was most definitely Leclerc," the stranger informed him calmly. "Or at least, the man I allowed people to think was Leclerc. He did everything I told him to. As did Ferris." He saw a momentary glimmer in Nicholas's eyes. "Yes, you know that name, don't you. And so you should. He was your leak, of course. I'm surprised old Osborne didn't stumble onto that one earlier. I was afraid he might have. Yes, both Ferris and Leclerc were very willing to go along with my plans…for the right price. They enabled me to operate undercover and completely above suspicion. I even let them believe that they were going to England. Pity you came along so soon."

Nicholas was finding it difficult to form words. His mouth didn't seem to want to work any more. "What do you…mean, pity?"

"I mean, dear boy, that if you hadn't stumbled along, I would have taken care of these two with no one any the wiser. No one would have discovered that Leclerc was not exactly who the British Intelligence thought he was—as illustrated by the picture I allowed to fall into Baker's hands—and I could have returned to London in complete safety. Even Ferris's duplicity would have gone undiscovered. He would have been hailed as a hero for being the one to kill the notorious French spy Jean Leclerc—sadly, just as Leclerc was killing him. You see, I couldn't risk either of them saying anything about me once they got to England. Just as I can't risk your going back to England now.'' His lips drew back in a malevolent sneer. ''As we both know, I have some…unfinished business to take care of.''

Nicholas took one look at the man's shadowy face and then lay back. ''Traitor!''

The word was little more than a gasp, and Nicholas dimly heard the sound of the man's scornful laughter. ''Such an unpleasant word, Nicholas, but yes, I suppose to you I would be. Still, I am sorry that we did not have the chance to meet on a more equal footing. I was looking forward to baiting you in Society, seeing if you could catch me out before I killed you. Now I fear it will be that much easier to dispatch the others—your own dear Lavinia included. Well, I think it is time I left. I hate watching a man in his death throes. Such an uncivilized sight, all that wretched blood. I'd much rather remember you as you were. Besides, I have a ship waiting to take me on a moonlit ride to the gently

rolling English countryside. And by this time tomorrow night, I shall be safely in London. *Adieu,*
Nicholas.''

Nicholas heard the man's mocking laughter, and
then the sound of the pistol being cocked. Drawing
on every last ounce of strength he possessed, he
twisted his body to the left at the precise moment
the gun fired, hoping it would be enough.

It wasn't.

Nicholas felt a searing pain in his head and then
the sound of laughter growing faint in the distance.
It was the last thing he was to remember before
everything went mercifully, painlessly, black.

SOMETHING WAS WRONG!

Lavinia stared at the cards in her hands and tried
not to cry out as the symbols suddenly became
blurred. She couldn't explain the feeling of fear
that had just come over her. She only knew she
was frightened. She began to shiver uncontrollably.

Beside her, Lady Torbarry crowed in delight.
''My hand again! I vow, I have never won so easily before, Lavinia. Wherever is your mind this
evening?'' The older woman turned towards her in
surprise. ''Lavinia? Are you all right, dear?''

Lavinia tried to smile, but found the effort more
than she could manage. ''I am sorry, Harriet. I'm
afraid my mind is really...not on my cards.'' Her

voice was wavering. "How much does that make it now?"

"Well, let me see." Lady Torbarry checked her calculations. "That brings the total to…fifty-six pounds you owe me."

Lavinia nodded, and rose rather unsteadily from the card table. "I shall have it sent round tomorrow. If you will excuse me…"

Before the woman had a chance to say anything else, Lavinia quit the card room and made her way back into the lavishly appointed gold salon. Her eyes scanned the room. She located Edward Kingsley across the floor and made for his side at once. "Edward, may I speak with you?"

Edward turned and gazed down into Lavinia's white face, the pleasant words of greeting he had been about to utter dying on his lips. Her breathing was shallow, and he could see the faint mist of perspiration on her forehead. "Lavinia, what's wrong?" he asked urgently.

"I…don't know." Lavinia closed her eyes. "Something has…happened."

Her breathing was becoming more erratic by the minute, and Edward recognized panic setting in. Excusing them both, he took Lavinia's arm and led her outside onto the balcony.

"Lavinia, listen to me," Edward said firmly.

"You're breathing too fast. You are going to pass out. Start taking deep, easy breaths."

Hearing the calming influence of his voice, Lavinia closed her eyes. She concentrated on her breathing, gradually bringing it back under control. The light-headedness passed.

"There, that's better," Edward said. "Now, what's happened to upset you so?"

Lavinia raised her troubled eyes to his. "I don't know. I was sitting playing cards with Lady Torbarry when this horrible feeling came over me."

Edward glanced at her sharply. "What kind of feeling?"

"I don't know. I can't explain it," she whispered. "Edward, I think something has happened…to Nicholas."

"Nicholas!" Edward stared at her in alarm. "What on earth are you talking about?"

Lavinia shook her head. "I know it doesn't make any sense, Edward, but I can't help what I feel, and I feel inside that something has gone very wrong. Nicholas has been hurt."

There was no doubting the depth of her fear, nor the strength of her conviction, and Edward thought for a moment. "Look, I think I had better take you home, Lavinia," he said finally. "And I'm going to have Laura stay with you."

"What are you going to do?"

"I'll see if I can get in touch with Osborne. Perhaps he's heard something."

Lavinia nodded in relief. "Thank you, Edward." She drew a shaky breath. "What if Nicholas has been…" She couldn't bring herself to say the words.

"He hasn't!" Edward said forcefully. "Now, come along. I'll have Laura fetch your cape. Shall I make your excuses?"

Lavinia nodded again. "I should be…grateful if you would."

An hour later, Lavinia and Laura sat together in the drawing-room of Lavinia's house, waiting for Edward to return. The nagging fear persisted, and no matter what she tried to do, Lavinia could not shake it. They had not woken Martine.

"But how do you know that something has happened, Lavinia?" Laura asked quietly. "Nicholas is hundreds of miles away."

Lavinia shook her head, her eyes staring into space. "I do not know, but I am certain that it has. I can feel it."

Laura bit her lip. "Do you know, it's strange, but Charlotte once told me that she and Edward had a…special bond. She told me that…she would know in her heart if something ever happened to him."

Lavinia nodded. "I never believed such things

possible, and I pray to God that I am mistaken, but I just felt—'' She broke off, her eyes turning to the door. ''Edward!'' She rose immediately. ''Well?''

Edward came in and shook his head regretfully. ''I'm sorry, Lavinia, but there's been no word. I told Osborne that you were…concerned, but there's really nothing we can do. The only thing we know for sure is that Nicholas was heading for Rosières, but that was days ago. There's been nothing from him since.''

Nothing from him since. The words rang in Lavinia's head like a death knell.

''We have to find him, Edward,'' she whispered, her lips white. ''He's been hurt, I know it. He's been hurt and he needs our help.'' She glanced up at Edward with pleading eyes. ''Please, tell Lord Osborne he must send help immediately!''

Edward glanced at Laura in concern. ''Osborne has already dispatched someone. If Nicholas is in trouble, we'll find him.''

Lavinia closed her eyes and leaned against Laura's shoulder. She would not cry. Not yet. Not while Nicholas needed her to be strong.

Don't leave me, Nicholas Lavinia cried silently. *You promised you would return. You have to come back!*

FROM SOMEWHERE FAR OFF in the distance, Nicholas heard a voice. It seemed to be the voice of an angel. Gentle and soft, it called to him, drawing him up out of his dark, dreamless sleep and forcing the gathering grey mists around him to part.

A heavy rain was falling. He felt the sting of drops against his face. He seemed to be lying in a ditch. He tried to move, but couldn't. His body felt stiff, numb. He couldn't feel his fingers. And there was a pain in his chest. Or was it in his leg?

Suddenly, a hand pressed gently against his forehead—a small, soft hand. And he heard a voice speaking to him. He struggled to open his eyes.

Was this what an angel looked like? Nicholas wondered, glancing up into a child's face surrounded by a halo of white-blond hair.

Her lips were moving, but he couldn't understand what she was saying. He was so hot. And so dreadfully thirsty.

''Pardon?'' He formed the word, but nothing came out. His throat was parched. Did he still have a voice? The angel started to move away.

No, don't leave me, he cried silently.

Surprisingly, she stayed. He saw that she was speaking again, or at least, that her lips were moving. Then Nicholas saw a movement at her side. A man. Nicholas sensed him moving around, and felt hands prodding his side. Agonizing pain shot through his body, stabbing his flesh like red-hot irons. Sweat broke out on his brow, and he felt the taste of blood in his mouth as he clamped down hard, stifling a scream. Again he felt the angel's comforting hands on his brow, but even that could do nothing to lessen his suffering.

Sometime later, he felt strong hands under his armpits. He felt the stiffness of wood being slid under his back, and then felt himself being lifted, the movement jarring his side. His mind screamed against the pain before he mercifully blacked out.

CHAPTER FOUR

"HE'S BEEN SHOT."

The words were spoken in a weary voice filled with bitter resignation. "I knew this would happen." Lord Osborne threw down the morning paper and glanced at Edward Kingsley in despair. "I should never have let Longworth go."

Edward studiously ignored the paper. "It isn't your fault, my lord. You couldn't have stopped him."

"Of course I could have stopped him. I *am* his commanding officer, damn it! I didn't allow him to go to France to rescue Lavinia Duplesse, and I shouldn't have allowed him to go after Leclerc, either." Osborne glanced at the paper in frustration. "Now I have to tell his fiancée that he's been shot, and that we have no idea where he is. Still, I suppose I should be thankful that he managed to get Leclerc."

"Yes. *And* the leak in the department."

"Ferris!" Osborne's nostrils quivered in anger.

"Never suspected him of being a double agent. Didn't think he had the stomach for it."

"Obviously he did. The fact that he and Leclerc were heading for the coast together proves they were collaborators."

"Well, they aren't any more." Osborne sat down at his desk and sighed heavily. "Both men dead by the hand of an unidentified assailant."

"Except that you and I know who that unidentified assailant was."

Osborne nodded. "All too well. I just wish I could bring myself to feel more pleased about this whole damn mess. All I can think about is that it was probably at the expense of Nicholas's life!"

The morning newspaper had been filled with the sensational story that suspected-French-spy Jean Leclerc and an Englishman travelling with him had been killed four nights ago, during what looked to have been a midnight robbery along the road to Calais. It seemed that the gendarmes had been advised of the accident by an anonymous letter. Upon arriving at the scene, they had found the bodies of Jean Leclerc, a man later identified as Andrew Ferris and a coachman. A paragraph at the end of the article briefly mentioned that a curate was also said to have been killed, but despite thorough investigation of the surrounding area, his body had not been found.

If nothing else, that small, seemingly inconsequential piece of news had given both Osborne and Kingsley the only glimmer of hope in an otherwise tragic report. They knew that Nicholas had been masquerading as a cleric. But it still left them no closer to knowing where he was now.

"How did the English papers get hold of the story, anyway?" Edward asked.

Osborne sighed. "We're not sure. I assume the same person who tipped off the French authorities must have slipped someone at *The Times* a note."

"What do you make of that?" Edward asked.

Osborne shrugged. "It could be that our informer was nothing more than an innocent passer-by travelling to the coast en route for England when he happened upon the accident."

"Then why is he so reluctant to make himself known?"

"Probably fears for his safety. The war isn't over yet."

Edward thought about that for a moment, but shook his head. "Something isn't making sense here, my lord. If the person who reported the accident knew that the priest was still alive, why didn't he stop to help the poor fellow? Conversely, if the priest was already dead, why was his body never found? Obviously, Nicholas was able to crawl off and find shelter, which means he could still be alive."

Osborne shook his head grimly. "I would like very much to think so, Kingsley, but according to the report, there was a great deal of blood on the grass at the edge of the wood, along with a bullet lodged in the mud. And Leclerc's pistol had been fired."

"Then where is Nicholas?" Edward asked. "A dead man doesn't just get up and walk away."

"No, he doesn't. Which is why I've dispatched Gordon to try to find him. I intend to do everything in my power to get Longworth back." Osborne stared sightlessly at the paper. "I refuse to believe he is dead until we have absolute proof of it."

HE WAS SURROUNDED by pain!

Nicholas stared into the shadowy darkness and clenched his fists against the terrible spasms that racked his body and made him gag. He began to shiver uncontrollably, even as the sweat poured off his body.

"Not...Leclerc," he gasped, eyes bright with fever as he tossed restlessly from side to side. "Not...Leclerc." Then, louder, "Lavinia... promise me...promise—"

The words broke off as the agonizing pain caught him, doubling him over. He felt gentle hands on his shoulders, forcing him back. His side was on fire. His whole body was on fire! He tasted the saltiness of sweat on his lips. "Water!" he gasped. "Water…"

Suddenly, the angel was there again. He felt the softness of her hand on his fevered brow as she pressed a water-soaked cloth to his lips. The cool liquid bathed the inside of his mouth and trickled down his throat.

"Lavinia!" he gasped, reaching for her blindly. His mind struggled to break through the suffocating haze. "I told you…I'd come back. I promised you—"

As the pain slashed through his side again like a red-hot knife, Nicholas groaned and fell back, his head rolling to the side as he slipped again into merciful unconsciousness.

LAVINIA SAT ON THE sofa in a delicate sprigged-muslin morning gown and tried to contain her anguish. The morning paper lay open on the sofa to one side of her. Edward sat patiently on the other.

"And you say the…cleric the paper mentions was actually…Nicholas," Lavinia intoned, her eyes fixed sightlessly on the window.

Edward nodded. "I am sorry to say that it was, Lavinia. Nicholas has used the cleric's outfit before, with great success. Osborne and I are convinced he was wearing it the night he was shot.''

Lavinia closed her eyes, as if to keep the painful words at bay. *The night he was shot!*

''So it was…Jean Leclerc who Nicholas went to find,'' she said. ''The man who…killed my husband.''

''Yes.''

''But why did Lord Osborne let him go?'' Lavinia whispered fiercely. ''If he knew the dangers, why didn't he send someone else? You told me yourself that neither you nor Nicholas could go to France to rescue me because your faces were too well known. Why did Lord Osborne suddenly change his mind and let Nicholas go now?''

''He didn't. Or at least, not willingly,'' Edward admitted. ''It was Nicholas who insisted upon going. Nicholas felt the only way of drawing Leclerc out was to send someone he would make an effort to…''

''Kill,'' Lavinia finished, when Edward did not.

''Lavinia, you must understand, Nicholas went because he knew the dangers—''

She made a strangled sound of disbelief. ''A lot of good it did him!''

''No, my dear, not the dangers in his going, the dangers in his *not* going,'' Edward corrected her gently. "The dangers in allowing Leclerc to come to England."

Lavinia raised her troubled eyes to his. "What dangers, Edward? The war is nearly over. Napoleon is banished. What dangers could possibly arise from a French agent being in London now?"

"Leclerc did not intend *his* war to end quite that easily, Lavinia." Edward chose his words with care. "We intercepted a letter the man sent to his superiors. In it, he detailed plans for returning to London after the war to...deal with certain people."

"What do you mean, deal with them?"

"To...silence them."

Lavinia paled. "Oh, my God, to kill them?"

"Yes."

"But why?"

"Because the man was a cold-blooded murderer."

Lavinia blanched, marvelling that anyone could be so evil. "Who was he intending to...deal with?" she asked tremulously.

"Certain people whom he'd encountered during the course of the war," Edward said evasively. "Enemies to the French cause. Naturally, when Nicholas learned of his intentions, he was determined to prevent Leclerc's coming to England, well aware that in an unsuspecting Society, a murderer like that would wreak havoc.''

Lavinia was silent for a moment. ''What of the people on this list, Edward? Was Nicholas one of them?''

Edward steeled himself to give the only answer he could. ''Yes.''

Lavinia's hands began to tremble. ''And you say Nicholas knew that?''

''He did.''

''Who else?''

''Myself, Lord Osborne, Lord Winchester, to name but a few.''

''Dear God!''

''Perhaps now you can better understand why Nicholas felt the urgency of going to France—to deal with Leclerc on his own ground.''

Lavinia struggled to come to terms with this new, highly disturbing information. Of course she could understand why Nicholas had felt so compelled to go to France. The lives of too many people had been at risk.

''But where is he now, Edward?'' she asked, gazing up at him intently. ''The cleric was supposedly shot, and yet his body was never found. Do you think it possible that Nicholas is still alive?''

''I do. Pardon me for speaking plainly, Lavinia,

but Nicholas is not the type to give up. If he wasn't killed outright by Leclerc's bullet—which, judging from the report, he was not—he will be doing everything he can to get back to England.''

"Then I must go to France," Lavinia said with quiet yet unshakable resolve. "He must be found. Until we hear otherwise, we must believe that Nicholas is alive."

"And we do, but there is certainly no question of your going to look for him," Edward said flatly. "It is far too dangerous."

"But don't you see, Edward? I must." Lavinia turned to gaze at him with pain-clouded eyes. "I can't just sit here waiting for news. I have to be there. Remember that night when I said that Nicholas was in danger?"

"Yes."

"Well, I was right. That was the night he was shot. I felt his pain, Edward. I knew he was suffering. And if I felt that, surely I would be able to feel if he was near me, and to find him. Dear God, Edward, I have to try!"

He could see that she was very close to breaking down, and he took her by the shoulders and shook her gently. "Now listen to me, Lavinia. I know you're worried about Nicholas. We all are. But your running off to France isn't going to help. Lord Osborne has already dispatched a man—a good man by the name of James Gordon. He will scour the area where Nicholas was last seen, and if he's alive, Gordon will bring him back. You have to trust me!''

''I do trust you,'' Lavinia said, still dreadfully near tears, ''but I can't just sit here and do nothing, Edward. I can't! I feel as though I am going mad as it is.''

''But you're not just sitting here doing nothing, my dear. You have Martine, and you cannot leave her alone,'' Edward said gently, knowing it was the only argument he could use that would mean anything to her. ''She is still getting over the death of her father and your own dangerous flight from France. The girl needs some stability in her life, Lavinia. She needs you. Only think what would happen to her if you were to go to France and meet with an accident.''

Lavinia stopped dead, her eyes widening. In her fear for Nicholas, she had momentarily forgotten about Martine, and was now overcome with a tremendous feeling of guilt at having done so. How could she have been so selfish? Martine had come to love and depend on her. She was the only family the girl now had. If something were to happen to her in France, how would Martine cope? Who could she turn to for comfort?

Yes, Edward was right, Lavinia conceded reluctantly. She would have to stay in England and wait for news. She had to be strong. Not just for her own sake, but for Martine's. She would have to wait until she heard the news that Nicholas was safe. But dear God, if only the waiting didn't hurt so much!

NICHOLAS SLOWLY OPENED his eyes, squinting slightly against the slivers of sunlight shining down through the barn boards above. The sound of birds chirping caused him to turn his head, as did the sound of a young girl humming somewhere below him.

Was it morning already? He must have fallen asleep. It had been dark the last time he remembered looking out. And he didn't feel as tired as he had. Even the excruciating throbbing in his side seemed to have eased a bit. But his head still felt sore and his mouth was dry as dust.

He went to sit up, but subsided with a moan. There was a stiffness around his middle. His exploring fingers located the presence of a wide bandage. "What the...?"

"Ah, *mon père,* you are awake at last!"

The soft French voice spoke gently in Nicholas's ear, and he turned in its direction. "You!"

It was the angel's face again. Pink and white,

with a cap of white-blond curls and a smile to make a man want to confess his worst sins.

"I 'ave brought you some of *maman's* broth," she said softly. "It will 'elp to make you strong."

Nicholas again tried to raise himself to a sitting position, and winced at the pain the movement caused him. "Damn!" He sank down weakly once more, before offering an apologetic, "Excuse me."

"It is of no concern. Here, perhaps you would like some water first?"

"Yes, very much." Nicholas glanced at his tiny nurse. She looked to be about eleven. "Who are you?"

The girl's smile was pure sunshine. "I am called Sophie. My brother and I found you lying injured in the road by my father's field."

Nicholas glanced at his surroundings with a total lack of comprehension. "Where am I? How did I...get here?"

"You are in my father's barn, and you are 'ere because my brother Antoine brought you in the cart. It was Antoine who took the bullet from your side and bandaged your head."

"Bullet?" Nicholas had a vague recollection of being shot, but his memory of the events leading up to it were hazy. "How long have I been here?" he asked quietly.

"A long time. Nine days, I think."

"Nine days!" he repeated incredulously.

Sophie nodded and lifted the cup to his lips. "Unfortunately, for most of them, you were unconscious with *la fièvre..* Now, drink slowly, *mon père.*"

Nicholas lifted his head and swallowed the water with some difficulty. Nine days. And most of the time delirious with fever. He shook his head in frustration. He didn't know how he had come to be here, or even where here was. In fact, he could remember nothing at all. Not even his own name.

"Do you want some soup?"

Nicholas nodded, and hesitantly opened his mouth as Sophie tipped a spoonful of the savoury broth into it. He swallowed tentatively, then looked at her and opened his mouth again.

Sophie smiled at him with pleasure. "It is good, *mon père*—you are eating again."

Nicholas glanced at her sharply. "Why do you call me *mon père*…Father?"

Sophie glanced at him curiously. "Because you wear the robes. And because you carry the missal. But you are English, *non?*"

Nicholas returned his attention to the soup. Strange. He knew that he was English, but he was also reasonably certain that he was not a man of the cloth. But if that was the case, what was he doing in robes? And why did he feel like his being

here was somehow endangering the lives of his
young nurse and her family?

"Sophie, I don't seem to be able to…think very
clearly right now, but I think it probably best that
I…leave as soon as possible," Nicholas said. "I
feel my being here is a…danger to you and your
family."

Sophie nodded a touch sadly. "*Oui,* I know. It
is fortunate that my father did not find you. 'E is
very suspicious of strangers. 'E probably would
not 'ave allowed us to help you, even though you
wore the robes. But Antoine is 'oping to be a doctor one day, and 'e said that a doctor does not turn
away from the sick, no matter who they are." Sophie looked proud. "Antoine is very smart."

"I am sure he is."

"I am glad that you did not die, *mon père.*"

Nicholas smiled in spite of his injuries. "You
saved my life, Sophie, and I shall never forget you
or your brother. In fact, I should very much like
to thank him if I could."

"It is not necessary." Sophie glanced towards
the door carefully, and then lowered her voice even
further. "There 'as been…a man looking for you.
An English, like you."

Nicholas gazed at her intently. "How do you
know that?"

"Antoine 'as 'eard the villagers speak of it."

Sophie leaned closer. "I believe this English is looking for you."

"For me?" Nicholas felt a swift rush of hope. "Is this man still in the area?"

"I do not know, but I can ask." Sophie watched the handsome Englishman, relieved that he had finally started to improve. "Would you like me to do that?"

Nicholas stared into the girl's face. He knew he didn't belong here. But where did he belong? He had to find out. And the man who was looking for him—did he know? He must. Why else would an Englishman be in the area? "Yes, Sophie, I would."

"Bon." Sophie rose and wrapped her shawl more closely about her shoulders. "I will ask Antoine to find out." She glanced at him almost sadly. "If the man is 'ere to take you away, you will want to go with 'im, yes?"

Nicholas nodded. "Yes, I think I probably should."

"D'accord." Sophie smiled bravely. "But until then, you must stay 'ere and rest. You are better than you were, but the wounds were very bad, *mon père,* and you lost much blood. Still, at least you are better off than the other men we found," she said with a noticeable shudder.

Nicholas glanced up at her in surprise. There

were other men? Who were they? And where were they now?

Nicholas knew he needed to ask those questions, but even as his mind framed the words, he felt himself drifting back to sleep. He was still so tired. His eyes were so heavy. "Yes, I…think perhaps I will…sleep, Sophie," Nicholas murmured.

Sophie watched him until he was asleep. Her eyes softened as she reached out to stroke his glistening black hair.

"Sleep well, *mon père,*" she said gently. "I will miss you." Then, taking one long, last look at him, Sophie left the barn to look for her brother in the far field.

WHAT HAPPENED OVER the next few days was little more than a blur in Longworth's mind. Gordon, the Englishman Sophie had told him about, said he had been sent by a Lord Osborne in London, and that he had been scouring the countryside. This news had come back to Nicholas via Sophie's brother, Antoine, just as it was through Antoine that arrangements were made for Nicholas to meet the Englishman after dark.

Nicholas bid a fond farewell to Sophie, knowing that she had saved his life. He kissed her cheek tenderly upon leaving, wishing he had something to give her. She had risked a great deal for him, she and her brother both.

"You are a very brave girl, Sophie," he said softly.

Sophie bravely held back her tears. "Goodbye, Monsieur Longworth." She had heard the other Englishman call him that name. "I 'ope you 'ave a safe journey back to England."

After thanking Antoine for all he had done, Longworth and the Englishman took their leave. James Gordon informed Nicholas that Lord Osborne had been searching high and low for him and that he would be mightily pleased to discover that he was still alive.

Nicholas smiled, but said nothing. It seemed decidedly ungrateful to say that he had no recollection whatsoever of the man who had obviously gone to so much trouble to find him.

THE TWO MEN MADE relatively good time. They travelled on horseback by night, preferring to seek cover in the heavy woods by day. Longworth was forced by the extent of his injuries to rest periodically, but he tried to keep each stop brief, aware that Gordon was anxious to be gone.

"'Tis dangerous country we be in, sir," Gordon said as they crouched together, eating sparingly of the food Sophie had managed to steal from her mother's kitchen. "The place is alive with Frenchies, all hunting for you."

"For me?" Nicholas shook his head in confusion. "But why? What have I done?"

Gordon gazed at him incredulously. "What have you done? Pardon me for saying so, sir, but you've bloody well done the impossible. Nobody thought Jean Leclerc could be brought down, and you did it single-handedly. Mind, Lord Osborne did say that if anyone was going to do it, you'd be the one. Damn proud he is, sir, damn proud. And I don't mind telling you, I'm honoured to be the man to bring you back. Just hope one of us lives to tell the tale!"

Three nights later, exhausted after a number of near encounters with roving French patrols, Gordon and Longworth crept down to a yacht moored at Le Havre and, under the cover of darkness, slipped out into the choppy waters of the English Channel.

Nicholas, wearied by the travelling and still very much troubled by his injuries, spent most of his time in his cabin resting. The thought of going back to a country of which he had no recollection—as well as to people who would be expecting him to remember them—was daunting, to say the least.

But if he was English, what had he been doing

in France? Gordon hadn't told him much, other than that he had brought this man Leclerc down. But who was Leclerc? And what nature of business had caused Nicholas himself to take two near-fatal bullets and be left at the side of the road to die?

He closed his eyes as the ship rolled with the waves. Going to England was like venturing into a new world—a world filled with faces he should know, but would not. How was he to explain that?

"LORD LONGWORTH, my lord."

The two gentlemen in the room slowly rose as Nicholas entered. He felt their eyes on him, studying him. He, in turn, glanced keenly from one to the other. The gentleman standing behind the desk was considerably older. Nicholas surmised that this must be the Lord Osborne Gordon had spoken of. He bowed slightly. "Lord Osborne, I presume."

He saw the man swallow. "Welcome home, Longworth." The man's voice was husky with emotion. "And may I commend you on a job well done. All England is proud of you."

Nicholas smiled vaguely. "Thank you, sir." He turned to address the other fellow, who looked to be more his own age, saying quietly, "Your servant, sir."

Edward's eyes never left Nicholas's face.

"Nicholas, do you not know me? I am Edward. Edward Kingsley."

Nicholas stared at the man's face, willing something, anything, to come back to him. But there was nothing—nothing but an empty, gaping hole where his past had been. "I wish I could say that I did, Mr....Kingsley, but the truth is—" Nicholas glanced at the older man apologetically "—I remember nothing."

As he stood and gazed at the two hopeful faces in front of him, Nicholas felt a sense of utter desolation. Nothing had changed. He did not recognize either of them. He gazed about this room with a complete lack of recognition. During the trip across the channel, he had harboured hopes that seeing familiar places and the people with whom he had shared his life might jog his memory in some fashion. But he realized now that such was not to be the case.

He cleared his throat awkwardly. "I feel I should...know you both, but I'm afraid..." His words drifted into silence.

Osborne swore and briefly turned away, the muscles in his jaw working. Edward's face filled with compassion. "Won't you...sit down, Lord Longworth?"

Nicholas started abruptly. "*Lord* Longworth?"

"You are Nicholas Grey, Viscount Longworth," Edward told him.

"Really? I didn't know." Nicholas smiled, almost as if in a daze. "Your man Gordon usually addressed me as 'sir'."

"Have you no memory of your life here at all?" Edward asked.

Nicholas cast his eyes about the room that he should have known, and regretfully shook his head. "None. It is as though I am seeing everything…for the first time."

Osborne had managed to get his emotions under control. He came around from behind his desk and sat down in the chair next to Nicholas.

"Can you tell us what happened, Nicholas? The night you were shot? Do you remember anything about it? Anything at all?"

Nicholas narrowed his eyes in concentration. He had gone over it in his mind time and again, helped along by what little information Sophie, her brother and James Gordon had been able to provide. "I remember almost nothing, my lord. I am told that there was…a carriage. And…a man. A Frenchman."

"Leclerc," Osborne supplied helpfully.

"Leclerc." Nicholas repeated the name experimentally. "Perhaps. But there was another man, too, I think. An…Englishman."

"Ferris," Edward added tersely. "He was travelling with Leclerc."

Nicholas glanced up hopefully. "Perhaps it would be possible to question them. They could tell us—"

"They are dead, Nicholas," Osborne informed him quietly. "You were forced to shoot them both. That is how you were wounded. Leclerc—or Ferris—shot you."

Nicholas stared at his commanding officer in astonishment. "I shot two men?"

"That was why you volunteered to go to France," Edward told him. "To get Leclerc."

"But what of the other Englishman?" Nicholas persisted, feeling instinctively that something was missing.

"You shot him, too," Osborne said, assuming Nicholas meant Ferris again. "He was the leak in the department. He was responsible for François Duplesse being murdered."

Nicholas looked confused. "François Duplesse?"

"Yes, Lavinia's—oh, my God," Edward muttered, glancing quickly at Osborne.

Nicholas saw the expression on the faces of both men and knew that something was horribly wrong. "What is it? Do I know this...François Duplesse?"

Osborne placed a hand gently on Nicholas's shoulder. "Not so much François as you do his widow, Lavinia."

"Do you remember Lavinia, Nicholas?" Edward asked, watching for some sign, however minute, of recognition.

"Lavinia." Nicholas said the name and then repeated it, but his expression remained blank. "I remember nothing." He lifted his eyes to Edward's face. "Should I know this lady?"

Edward sighed, more heartsick than he could ever remember having felt in his life. "Yes, my friend, you know this lady. She is the woman you are engaged to marry."

CHAPTER FIVE

LAVINIA STOOD BY the window, anxiously watching for the carriage. She knew that they were coming. Edward had stopped by the house last night and told her. He had also told her, as gently as possible, that her fiancé had absolutely no memory of his previous life in London—or of her. When they met again, it would be for Nicholas like the very first time.

Lavinia had hid her grief remarkably well. She had waited until Edward had gone before breaking down and shedding heart-wrenching tears in the privacy of her room. She had railed against God for taking away Nicholas's memory, and then, in the same breath, had thanked Him for sparing his life.

After all, where there was life, there was hope, Lavinia told herself firmly. As long as Nicholas was alive, there was a chance that his memory would return. Dear God, it had to return!

The sound of a carriage in the street below drew Lavinia's attention back to the window. She watched the curricle pull up and then caught her breath as two gentlemen got out.

Nicholas!

As if hearing her silent cry, he glanced up towards the window and looked at her. Her heart turned over at the sight of his beloved face, the same moment as her hand went to her mouth to stifle the sob. He had not recognized her.

"Lord Longworth and Mr. Kingsley," Habinger announced solemnly a few minutes later.

Lavinia was unaware that she was still holding her breath. Her eyes went immediately to Nicholas, taking in the dreadful pallor of his skin. His face was more drawn than she had ever seen it, no doubt as a result of his injuries. He moved stiffly, as though the wound in his side still pained him. But it was the look in his eyes that troubled her the most.

There was nothing there—no flicker of recognition, no warm glow of love. No spark at seeing her again—the woman he had professed to love.

"Nicholas!" she murmured huskily.

Nicholas advanced uncertainly into the tastefully decorated room, thankful for Edward's presence at his side.

"Nicholas, this is Lavinia, Lady Duplesse," Edward said softly. "Now, I am going to leave the two of you alone for a few minutes, all right? I'll be just outside if you need me.''

"Thank you, Edward," Lavinia said.

Nicholas nodded. As the door closed behind Edward, he turned back towards the beautiful woman in front of him, seeing the hope in her eyes, and he felt sorrow so deep it made him want to run from the room.

"I am so very, very sorry," he whispered, his throat husky with emotion. "I know that I should...know you, but—"

Lavinia caught her breath and felt the swift rush of tears to her eyes. She had promised herself that she would not cry again, but seeing him now, like this, it was so very hard not to.

"No, Nicholas, you have no need to apologize. It is...not your fault. But please, if you would just...hold me for a moment."

Nicholas slowly opened his arms and Lavinia walked into them. He felt the warmth and the softness of her body as she pressed against him, and his arms closed automatically around her. She smelled of violets, sweet and undeniably feminine. Dear God, he had been about to marry this beautiful creature?

Lavinia allowed herself a few moments of pure bliss in the circle of Nicholas's arms. She knew he did not remember her, but right now, that didn't matter. All that mattered was that he was alive. He was safe, and they were together again. At the moment, that was all she had.

Forcing herself to smile, Lavinia reluctantly stepped out of his arms, hastily wiping away a tear that managed to escape and trickle down her cheek.

"Please, do not cry for me, Lavinia," Nicholas said suddenly.

Lavinia thought she had her emotions under control, but the softness in his voice proved to be her undoing. She abruptly turned away, unable to halt the flow of tears, while Nicholas stood helplessly by, his hands clenched uselessly at his side. He wanted to comfort her, but he didn't know how. It seemed that his presence was only upsetting her more. "Perhaps I should leave?"

"No!" Lavinia spun around, her cheeks streaked with tears. Then, more softly, she added, "No, Nicholas, please…do not leave. Forgive me, I did not mean to cry." She took a deep breath and managed a shaky laugh. "I promised myself I would not, but when I heard your voice…when you held me…" She cleared her throat and gestured towards a chair. "Won't you…sit down?"

"Thank you."

Nicholas sat down slowly, his eyes never leaving her face. She was an incredibly beautiful woman. Even in grief, her loveliness was undiminished. The pale lavender gown did little to hide the womanly curves beneath. Her dark, glistening hair was drawn up into an elegant chignon, her complexion was smooth, her lips reminiscent of a dusky rose.

Yes, she was beautiful, but there was also an underlying strength that Nicholas felt as surely as though it lay open and exposed to him. This was an admirable woman—a woman who had known pain and suffering and who had come through it. An admirable woman, his Lavinia.

His Lavinia. Unbidden, his eyes went to the ring on her left hand.

"Yes, my lord, we are…betrothed," Lavinia said, noting his regard. "Or rather, we were," she said uncertainly.

"I must have been considered a very fortunate man," Nicholas said quietly. "Though given the circumstances, I can understand your wishing to…withdraw your promise."

Lavinia swallowed, trying not to show how deeply his innocent words had hurt her. "Nicholas, I know that…much has happened to you. But you must understand that…my feelings…have not changed in any way. You are still the man I fell in love with, and the man with whom I am in love still."

Nicholas watched the play of emotions across

her face. "Edward told me very briefly what happened in our pasts. It would appear that…I have always loved you."

Lavinia smiled. "Yes. We have been through a great deal, you and I."

"But what of us now?" Nicholas asked, knowing that he had to ask, and as soon as possible. "You see that I have no memory of what went before. I know that Edward hoped my seeing you might trigger something in my memory. Indeed, I had hoped it myself, for I confess I have never felt so lost in my life. But now that I have seen you, and realize that I have absolutely no recollection of…what has passed between us, would you not choose to be free? To start your life again? Surely you would not have yourself shackled to someone who is but a ghost from the past. You are young and beautiful. You must have admirers by the score."

Lavinia shook her head. "I care not if I have, Nicholas. You are the only man I have ever loved, and your accident has not changed that. In fact, I have no desire to change anything at the moment."

Impulsively, she crossed to his chair. Lowering herself to the carpet at his feet, she took one of his hands and held it tightly between her own. "I will ask nothing of you, Nicholas, and expect nothing in return. But perhaps, in some way, I can help you.''

''Help me? How?''

''By leading you through the steps of your life as it was,'' Lavinia said quietly. ''Perhaps by meeting people and seeing things that were once part of your life, your memory will return.''

Nicholas closed his eyes. ''I wish with all my heart that it might happen, Lavinia, but I cannot know for sure if it will. The doctor Lord Osborne arranged for me to see told me that my memory may never come back.'' He opened his eyes and looked down into her face. ''Will it not be terribly difficult for you? I cannot lie and tell you that…things are…as they were between us.''

''I realize that you no longer…love me, Nicholas,'' Lavinia forced herself to say. ''How can you, when you have no recollection of who I am? But because of what I once was to you, and because of what you still are to me, I would try.'' She gave a shaky laugh. ''God knows, I have little enough to lose by trying, and everything to gain.''

Nicholas gazed down at her intently. Then he smiled. ''I think I must have been an intelligent man to have chosen such an admirable woman to be my wife.'' He paused and then came to a decision. ''All right, Lavinia, if it is truly what you wish. I see no reason to end our betrothal right now, and I would be heartily grateful for your help.''

Lavinia saw his gaze drop to her mouth, and felt a familiar flutter in her stomach. ''Was there something else you wanted to say, Nicholas?'' she asked tentatively.

''Not say, exactly,'' he murmured. Slowly, as if unsure of her reaction, Nicholas leaned forward. Would he remember how she felt, perhaps? He lifted one hand and ran his thumb along the edge of her cheek, along her jaw. He could see the flickering pulse in the tender hollow at the base of her throat.

Slowly raising her to her knees, Nicholas pulled her closer. He saw her eyes close, and she swayed towards him almost unconsciously, her beautiful lips slightly parted...

''Hello, I hope I'm not—oh, pardon me!'' Edward broke off abruptly, pausing with his head around the door. ''It would appear that I am indeed interrupting.''

Lavinia hastily opened her eyes as Nicholas drew back awkwardly. She noticed that she wasn't the only one blushing.

''No, it's...quite all right, Edward.'' Lavinia was the first to regain her composure. She rose gracefully to her feet. ''Come in.''

''I say,'' Edward said, glancing from one to the

other hopefully. "Things are looking very good between the two of you. Have you remembered something, Nicholas?"

Nicholas shook his head, more confused and upset than he could ever remember having felt in his life. He had wanted to kiss Lavinia Duplesse very much just now, but he wasn't sure why. Apart from the fact that she was an extremely beautiful woman, she meant nothing to him.

"No, I fear not. Lavinia and I were just... discussing our engagement."

Edward's face creased in a smile. "Rather nice way of discussing it, that," he said, winking at Nicholas. "Well, what have the two of you decided?"

"That there is no need to break off our betrothal just yet," Lavinia informed him quietly. She turned to smile at her fiancé. "Nicholas has agreed to allow me to help him go about his daily routine. Perhaps by doing so, we will be able to jog something in his memory."

"Well, I am very glad to hear that." There was no denying the relief in Edward's voice. "The doctor did say that the memory lapse might not be permanent. Perhaps all it will take is some trifling detail, some inconsequential act, to bring it back again."

"I sincerely hope so," Nicholas said. He

glanced at Lavinia, and at length, he smiled. "It would seem that I have a very good reason for wanting it to return."

Lavinia blushed, immeasurably pleased that he would say so. But as she bid him goodbye a little while later, one thing became very clear in her mind. From this moment on, she intended to work very hard at helping Nicholas remember. He was everything in the world to her, and if it took the rest of her life, she would make his memory return.

Either that, or she would make him fall in love with her again!

So BEGAN NICHOLAS'S gentle reintroduction to the life he had led before the mission to France robbed him of his memory. The knowledge that he had been the one to kill the notorious French spy, Jean Leclerc, spread quickly, and his reception was that of a returning hero. Unfortunately, the fact that Nicholas had no recollection of his former life, nor of what he had done in France, quickly put a damper on his reunion with the people that he met.

"No one seems to know what to say to him," Lavinia complained to Laura Beaufort two days later, as they sat together in the front parlour of Lavinia's house. "Nicholas and I went driving this afternoon, and though people were happy enough to smile and nod at him, very few approached us, even though he is perfectly charming to everyone.''

Laura sighed. ''Poor man. I cannot imagine what it must be like to return to a place I have lived all my life and not know a soul. How dreadfully lonely it must be for him.''

Lavinia nodded. She knew the strain Nicholas was under. It was as though he was isolated from everything, from everyone. He held on to both Lavinia and Edward now as though they were his lifelines.

''Have you reintroduced him to Martine yet?''

''I haven't even told him about her. I'm trying not to thrust too much upon him at once. Coming back to London and finding out that he was engaged to be married was one thing, but telling him that he is about to become a stepfather as well...'' Lavinia laughed and shook her head. ''I could not bring myself to do it. Besides, Nicholas has been spending a good deal of time with Lord Osborne, and on the two occasions he has been here, Martine was out with a friend. But I have invited Nicholas to call round tomorrow afternoon. Martine will meet him then.''

''Is she aware of what happened?'' Laura enquired softly.

''Yes. I thought it only fair that she know before Nicholas arrived. She did not say very much the whole time Nicholas was gone, but I knew she was worried. And I am very pleased at how well she took the news of his memory loss.''

"What of his mother?" Laura asked now. "Has she been to see him?"

Lavinia bit her lip. "We are going to see her this evening, in fact. I received a note from her, asking us to call."

Laura raised an eyebrow in surprise. "Both of you?"

"Yes. Surprising, is it not?"

"Promising, more like." Laura was well aware that Lady Longworth did not hold Lavinia in the greatest of affection. "Perhaps she is mellowing towards you."

Lavinia could only hope that it was true. But in the carriage on the way to Lady Longworth's later that evening, she truly began to wonder. After all, if Lady Longworth knew that her son had been injured as a result of an altercation with the man who had killed her first husband, was she not likely to hold Lavinia in even greater contempt? It seemed a logical assumption. For that reason, Lavinia could only hope that the true identity of Jean Leclerc was never made known to her.

Lavinia felt the growing tension in Nicholas's body. "Nicholas, what's wrong?"

He shook his head. "Nothing. Other than that it

seems incredible that I should have no memory of my own mother.'' He turned and glanced at her thoughtfully. ''What is she like?''

''Your mother? Well, she is…a most dignified lady,'' Lavinia said, anxious to present the woman in a positive light. ''And quite a handsome woman…for her age.''

''No, no, I meant her character,'' Nicholas said. ''Were we close?''

Oh dear, Lavinia groaned inwardly. How honest should she be?

''I cannot say that you were…close, precisely. You did not see…a great deal of each other,'' she answered tactfully.

Nicholas nodded thoughtfully. ''I see. And what about you?''

''Me?''

''Yes. Did you like my mother?'' he asked innocently. ''Was she happy that we were to be married?''

Lavinia bit her lip. This was getting decidedly difficult.

''No, Nicholas, your mother and I were not exactly close,'' she said finally, deciding that honesty—without too much explanation—was probably the best policy. ''But then, we have not spent a great deal of time together. I was just recently out of mourning for my husband, you see, and not given to socializing much.''

''But surely she was pleased that we were to be married?'' he persisted.

''I cannot say that your mother ever told me to my face that she was not.''

''Ah. Then I imagine she will be happy to hear that we have decided not to break off our betrothal,'' Nicholas said with some satisfaction.

''Yes, I daresay she will have something to say about that,'' Lavinia murmured.

They were greeted at the door by Lady Longworth's butler and then shown into the drawing-room, where a warm fire burned in the grate. Nicholas walked around the perimeter of the spacious room, touching objects, studying the furniture and the decorations. ''Was I here recently?'' he enquired.

Lavinia nodded. ''Shortly before you left. You and your mother had dinner together.''

''How strange that I have no recollection of it whatsoever.'' Nicholas's attention was momentarily arrested by the large painting over the fireplace. ''Was that my father?''

''It was,'' a voice answered from the doorway. ''Two years before he died.''

They both turned as the Dowager Lady Longworth walked into the room. Lavinia curtsied out of respect, but she had a feeling the woman never even saw her. Lady Longworth went straight to her son and stared up into his face. "Is it true, what I have been hearing?" she asked quietly. "You have no recollection of the past?"

Nicholas shook his head. "It is true." He gazed down into the face of the woman who had given him birth, and felt a blinding return of despair. "I do not even remember you."

Lady Longworth closed her eyes, an inarticulate sound escaping her lips as grief welled up in her. *"I am your mother."*

Nicholas swallowed, and gently brushed her cheek with his lips, paying her the homage he knew was due. "Yes, I know. Forgive me."

He straightened, and the two regarded each other in silence. Lady Longworth shook her head. "It is not for you to ask forgiveness, Nicholas. This is not your fault. Nor had I the right to criticize you, since I now understand why you went." She glanced briefly at Lavinia, her blue eyes chilly, but uncertain. "Did he remember you?"

"No. Mr. Kingsley told him who I was."

Lavinia expected to see a look of satisfaction appear on the old woman's face. Instead, all she saw was a great sadness. "Then am I to assume that your engagement is no longer in place?"

"No, Mother," Nicholas said. "For the moment, we saw no need to end it. The doctors said that the memory loss may be temporary, and that by continuously seeing things that were part of my life, I may suddenly remember something. Lavinia has kindly offered to stay and help me work through this.''

Lady Longworth looked at Lavinia with grudging respect. "It is…good of you, Lady Duplesse. It cannot be easy."

Lavinia shook her head in surprise, recognizing that the woman was making an effort. "It is not, Lady Longworth. But I continue to hope."

"Come, let us sit down. Nicholas, why don't you sit here by the fire. I will have Mortimer build it up a bit. The evening is chilly."

"It is quite all right for me…Mother. I do not seem to feel the cold much."

His mother hesitated uncertainly. "Well, if you are sure."

The three of them sat down, Lady Longworth in her usual chair by the fire, Lavinia and Nicholas together on the sofa.

"So, Nicholas, you have earned yourself a hero's welcome." Lady Longworth nodded. "I am proud of you. Though I wish to God you had never gone to France. Was it so important, your finding this man—what was his name—Leclerc?"

Nicholas smiled. "I am told that it was, though

I cannot honestly recall my reasons for having gone. Perhaps if I could, I would feel more settled in my own mind. Lord Osborne told me that what I did was of great importance, and that many lives were saved."

Lady Longworth watched him sadly. "But at such great cost, Nicholas. At such great cost."

Nicholas smiled, and strove for a measure of lightness in his voice. "It is not so bad, Mother. I have an opportunity to begin again. Every day is a great adventure. And every day I wake hoping this might be the day it all comes back to me."

Lady Longworth was not so easily mollified. "And you remember nothing of me? Of your father? Your life here?"

Nicholas's smile faded. "No." He paused. "Sometimes I think I am just beginning to grasp something, only to have it…disappear seconds later."

A heavy silence fell, broken only by the crackling of the logs in the fireplace.

"I understand you have a daughter, Lady Duplesse," Lady Longworth said unexpectedly, rousing herself. "How is she adjusting to life in London?"

"Very well, thank you, my lady," Lavinia answered. "It is all a bit strange to her, of course, but I am very pleased with the progress she is making.''

''You have a daughter?''

Lavinia turned towards Nicholas, a fresh stab of pain twisting in her heart at the look of surprise in his eyes. ''A stepdaughter, actually. Martine is François's child.''

''Martine.'' Nicholas repeated the name, as he always did when a new name was mentioned. ''How old is…Martine?''

''She is seventeen.''

''Seventeen!'' Nicholas continued to look dazed. ''Why have you not told me about her?''

Lavinia blushed uncomfortably. ''I thought it…better to wait, Nicholas. You had enough to come to terms with. But you will be meeting her tomorrow. That is why I asked you to call.''

Nicholas nodded, mulling things over in his mind. ''How long were you and your husband married?''

''Four years.''

''I see. Then…how did I come to meet you?''

''You met Lady Duplesse at her wedding, Nicholas,'' Lady Longworth informed her son quietly.

There was no resentment in the woman's voice, and Lavinia glanced at her hesitantly. ''I truly wish it had been sooner, Lady Longworth,'' Lavinia told her softly.

She was amazed to see a thawing in the blue eyes and the appearance of a tentative smile. "Yes, I realize that now, Lady Duplesse." She turned to look almost gratefully, Lavinia thought, at her son. "It would seem that I have, indeed, been given another chance to realize that."

THE EVENING PASSED pleasantly enough, but by the end of it, Lavinia was more than ready to leave. It had been a strain on everyone, especially Nicholas. She had watched him all evening as he struggled to remember the names his mother mentioned, the places they had been and the things they had done as a family.

Still, it was not a complete loss, Lavinia reflected. At least she and Lady Longworth appeared to have made some headway with their own relationship.

"You are uncommonly quiet, my lord," Lavinia said in the carriage on the way home.

Nicholas breathed a heavy sigh. "It is so strange, seeing someone like…my mother. Knowing that there should be so many memories, yet having none. And I could see it was difficult for her." His next remark surprised her. "We were not close, were we."

Lavinia glanced at him sharply. He hadn't

phrased it as a question. "Why would you say that, Nicholas?"

"Because I felt it. I felt…the reserve. It shouldn't have been there, but it was."

"Perhaps she just did not know what to say to you."

Nicholas shook his head sadly. "No, Lavinia. People I meet on the street do not know what to say to me. Acquaintances I see in the Park do not know what to say to me. My mother did not know *how* to speak to me, and therein lies the difference." He offered her a weak smile. "I may not remember much about my own life, but I do know the way it should be between a mother and son."

Lavinia had to fight the urge to pull him into her arms and comfort him. There was so much loneliness in him. So much emptiness. And loving him the way she did it made it that much harder to bear. It tore at her soul, making her feel empty as well. There was so much she wanted him to know, and so much she wanted to tell him.

"Nicholas, how would you like to go down to the country for a while?"

Nicholas glanced at her in surprise. "The country?"

"Yes, I think it might be a good idea."

"Do I have a house in the country?" Nicholas enquired.

Lavinia managed a laugh. "Yes, of course you do, but actually, I was thinking of my own. I have a house in Kent. I haven't been there in years, but it could be made ready for us in a few days." As she was speaking, Lavinia found herself warming to the idea. "Perhaps it would be good for you to get out of London for a while."

Nicholas sighed. "I confess, I am growing weary of people staring at me as though I were an imbecile."

Lavinia rushed to his defence. "They are not looking at you that way at all, Nicholas. It is merely that they are...unsure as to how to approach you."

Unexpectedly, he lifted her hand to his lips and pressed a kiss into her soft palm. "Would that they all had your tact and patience, Lavinia."

Lavinia felt the tears spring to her eyes. "Ah, but they do not love you the way I do," she replied, striving for a bantering tone.

The look he turned towards her was laden with sadness. "Am I not beginning to wear on your patience, too, Lavinia? God knows, you have reason to feel that way."

"You could never try my patience, Nicholas. I *love* you. Nothing in the world is more important to me than you. You must believe that."

He nodded slowly, and then his eyes darkened

as he looked at her. He suddenly felt an inexplicable longing to be close to her.

"Lavinia, I have no wish to embarrass you, but…were we ever…that is, did we ever…" The words trailed off.

Lavinia knew what he was trying to say, and resisted the urge to smile. "No, we…never did. Why would you ask?"

"Because I cannot help but be strongly aware of you…as a woman, and I simply wondered if there was…a reason for it."

Lavinia was thankful the darkness of the carriage hid her flaming cheeks. "No, Nicholas, we were never…intimate, though there were times when we came rather close."

He smiled at her in the darkness. "How close?"

She laughed unsteadily. "Very close, though you always stopped before things went too far."

She heard him sigh. "Always the gentleman, eh?"

"Well, perhaps not…all the time," Lavinia admitted, blushing hotly. "There was…one occasion where I had to tell you to behave."

Nicholas turned, his smile widening. "Really?"

"Twice, in fact."

"Good Lord, twice? Whatever was I doing?"

"Nicholas, I really don't think—"

"No, you must tell me, Lavinia," he said, endeavouring to keep a straight face. "After all, the doctor did say that it was impossible to tell what might prompt me into remembering."

Lavinia glanced down at her hands. "Really, Nicholas, I hardly think something as...trivial as this would initiate a complete return of your memory."

His laugh was low and disturbingly sensual. "Why don't you try me?"

Lavinia's cheeks grew warmer. "Well, if you must know...it was on the day after you...proposed to me."

"The day after?"

"Yes. We had just come back from dinner at the Clarendon Hotel, where you had taken me to celebrate our betrothal. You had engaged a private chamber."

"How romantic of me," Nicholas said with a chuckle.

"Oh, yes, it was certainly that. Needless to say, I was very impressed, Lord Longworth."

"I am delighted to hear it. So how did I blot my copybook after starting out so well?"

"When you brought me home, I invited you in for a glass of brandy."

"All very honest and above-board," Nicholas observed.

"Yes, it was. Except that one glass stretched to

two, and given that you had already imbibed rather freely at dinner, well, you ended up being a little more…amorous than usual.''

His mouth quirked with humour. ''Is that when you were forced to tell me to behave?''

''Yes, I'm afraid it was. You became rather…fascinated with the beadwork on my gown. Especially on the…bodice of my gown.''

Unbidden, Nicholas's dark eyes dropped to the soft swell of Lavinia's breasts, now safely hidden beneath her elegant pelisse. A delightful picture formed in his mind. ''I take it you were wearing a low-cut gown?'' He was surprised to hear the huskiness in his voice.

Lavinia bit her lip and tried not to laugh. ''Shockingly low, I'm afraid. And you were rather intent on seeing how the beads were attached to the…inside of the fabric.''

Nicholas purposely cleared his throat, wondering why he couldn't clear away the image in his mind. He shifted uncomfortably in his seat, aware of a tightening in his lower body. ''I hope I apologized for my disreputable behaviour the next morning.''

This time, Lavinia couldn't help but laugh. ''Yes, you certainly did. In fact, you were so busy apologizing I never did get a chance to tell you that I…really wasn't annoyed at all.''

Nicholas stared at her in astonishment. "You weren't?"

"No. Now," Lavinia said, suddenly sounding prim, "I do believe we were talking about going down to the country, were we not?"

Nicholas let out his breath. "Yes," he muttered faintly, "I do believe we were."

LAVINIA WAS DELIGHTED at how well Nicholas responded to Martine the following afternoon. She had feared that an awkwardness might develop between them, but it was only moments before she realized that she had absolutely no cause for concern. Martine accepted Nicholas's reserve and quickly broke it down. There was no discomfort or embarrassment at all. In fact, Nicholas appeared far more at ease in the company of the seventeen-year-old French girl than he did with many of his tonnish friends.

Lavinia had received an invitation to her good friend Lady Renton's musicale while Nicholas was still in France. The invitation had been extended to both of them, of course, and Lavinia thought it might be a good opportunity for Nicholas to attend his first social function since returning to London. But when she mentioned it to him that afternoon, she was not overly surprised when he demurred.

"You are not angry, I hope?" he asked quickly.

Lavinia shook her head. "No, of course not. There will be other functions, Nicholas."

"Will Lady Renton be offended?" he enquired tactfully.

"Not in the least. Caroline is a close friend of mine. She will not expect a long explanation, nor will I feel obliged to give one."

"I am relieved." Nicholas hesitated. "Is there perhaps another gentleman you might like to have accompany you?"

Lavinia laughed in delight and relief. "No, and I am happy to say that one of the advantages of being a widow is that I am allowed a great deal more freedom than I ever had before. It is not necessary that I be escorted to every function."

And it was true enough. Lavinia went to the musicale quite comfortably on her own. She probably would not have gone at all, except for the fact that her dear friend Lady Renton was holding it. The two had been friends since school, and had spent a great deal of time since Lavinia's return catching up on their years apart. Lady Renton—Caroline Abbott before her marriage—was one of the few people Lavinia had troubled to keep in touch with, even during her time in France.

"And you say he remembers nothing?" Lady Renton asked after the Italian tenor finished sing-

ing and the two friends had strolled into the ball-
room, where refreshments were being served.

"Nothing. Names, faces—they mean nothing to
him," Lavinia told her sadly. "I don't know that
he even remembers places. He did not seem to recognize my parlour."

Lady Renton laughed. "Dear me, perhaps you
should have taken him up to your boudoir, Livie.
That might have jogged his memory."

"Caroline!" Lavinia gasped, blushing and
laughing all at once. "Nicholas has never been in
my...boudoir."

"No? Pity. Handsome man like that. I thought
you might not have been able to resist the temp-
tation. After all, my dear, you are a widow."

"I know, Caroline, but that does not give me
licence to act disrespectfully."

"Tosh, Livie, how disrespectful would it have
been?" Caroline's face was surprisingly compas-
sionate. "Everyone knows how dreadfully in love
the two of you were. How can you feel that kind
of love and not wish to..."

Lavinia blushed again. "I'm not saying I did not
wish to, Caroline," she admitted, biting her lip. "I
am merely saying that we never...did."

"Hmm. Well, more's the pity," Caroline observed. "It might have helped jog his memory.

Great things have been known to happen in the midst of passion, you know.''

"I shall try to remember that," Lavinia said drily.

"Excuse me, Lady Renton, but I wonder if I might have a word.''

Both ladies turned at the sound of a deep, masculine voice, and Lavinia found herself looking into the faces of two men she could not recall having seen before.

One was quite tall and very elegantly, though not foppishly, dressed. He appeared to Lavinia somewhat older than many of the men present, and yet was still exceedingly handsome. The man standing beside him was equally well-dressed. His chestnut brown hair was cropped short in the back and brushed forward in the current style.

"Ah, Lord Rushton, Lord Havermere, how good of you both to come," Caroline said warmly. "I was not sure you were returned to London.''

The man identified as Lord Havermere bowed. "We are only recently returned, my lady, having spent the last few weeks at my estate in the north of Scotland. But we were most grateful for your invitation.''

"And I am delighted you could come." Caroline turned towards Lavinia. "May I introduce my good friend, Lady Duplesse. Lavinia, Lord Havermere, and Lord Rushton.''

Lord Rushton smiled in an urbane manner. "So we finally meet, Lady Duplesse. I knew your husband."

Lavinia glanced at him in surprise. "You did?"

"Yes, although it was many years ago. We attended the Sorbonne together."

"You do not look old enough to have been a classmate of my husband's, Lord Rushton."

Rushton's voice was perfectly cultured, though somewhat lacking in inflection. "You flatter me, Lady Duplesse. I assure you, only a few years separated us in age."

"I understand you are engaged to be married, Lady Duplesse," Lord Havermere said now.

Lavinia managed a smile. "Yes, I am."

"Is your fiancé here this evening?"

"Sadly, he was feeling a trifle indisposed."

"Lady Duplesse is engaged to Lord Longworth, my lord," Caroline said quickly. "He is only recently returned to London after suffering an illness on the Continent. He has not yet taken up the rounds of Society."

"Ah, yes, now I remember," Havermere said. He turned back towards Lavinia. "Something about an accident in France."

"Yes."

"Dreadful shame. I understand he was very ill. And something about him...losing his memory, if I remember correctly?"

"Yes, that's right."

"What a pity," Lord Rushton remarked. "Has he no memory at all?"

"None, I'm afraid."

"Dear me, what an inconvenience," Havermere remarked in a sympathetic tone. "I can't imagine what it must be like not to remember places and names. Please extend our condolences, Lady Duplesse."

"Yes, thank you, I shall."

"Oh, Lavinia, will you excuse me?" Caroline said suddenly. "I see Lady Stanton gesturing madly. No doubt we have run out of some delicacy she is partial to. Gentlemen, please do continue to enjoy yourselves."

"We are sure to, Lady Renton," Lord Havermere replied smoothly.

When Caroline had gone, Lavinia turned to find Lord Rushton watching her speculatively. "My lord?"

"Forgive me, Lady Duplesse. I did not mean to stare. I was just thinking what a shame it is, Lord Longworth losing his memory like that, coming back to London and finding everything suddenly a mystery."

Lavinia smiled bravely. "Indeed, it is a shame, but he is managing extremely well."

"I am sure he is. And you say he remembers nothing at all of what happened?"

"Nothing."

Lord Havermere shook his head. "Do the doctors hold out any hope?"

"They cannot say. Apparently, Nicholas was very ill. He nearly died. I suppose we should be thankful that it was only his memory he lost."

"Yes, of course," Havermere replied. "Still, it must be a comfort to him that he was able to take care of that blackguard Leclerc before being wounded himself."

It was on the tip of Lavinia's tongue to ask him how he knew about Leclerc, but then she remembered that the account of the incident had been well detailed in the newspaper. No doubt everyone in London knew what had happened on that terrible night in France.

"Nasty business," Rushton was continuing, as if following her thoughts. "For myself, I shall be glad when the war is over. All this cloak-and-dagger nonsense—it leaves one wondering whom you can really trust, does it not, Lady Duplesse?"

Lavinia could not explain why the presence of the two men made her feel ill at ease. There was really nothing objectionable about either of them.

They were both well spoken and very distinguished looking. So what was it about them that made Lavinia want to put as much distance between herself and them as possible?

CHAPTER SIX

LAVINIA DECIDED THAT they would go down to the country in a week's time. She felt the days in between would give the staff at the house in Kent time to get ready, as well as give Nicholas plenty of time to accustom himself to the idea. She told Edward Kingsley of her intention, and was relieved to receive his overwhelming approval.

"I think it's a splendid idea," Edward replied honestly. "Nicholas is trying too hard here. Every time he looks at something new, he is forcing himself to remember. Truth is, he's putting more strain on himself than is good for him."

"I thought much the same," Lavinia confided. "I am hoping that the peace and quiet of Rose Cottage will bring some peace to his soul. Lord knows, he seems to have little enough of it now."

And it was true. Rather than becoming more accustomed to his lack of memory, Nicholas was growing more distressed by it. He found himself falling into a temper far faster than before. He became impatient with himself and with those around him. And he knew why.

The suspicion that something had gone wrong in France would not leave him. It remained like a troublesome thorn in his side—there, but just out of reach. He knew now, after having spoken at length with Lord Osborne, exactly what he had gone over to do and why. He now understood that this man Leclerc had planned to return to England, and that he had threatened to kill certain people once he arrived. Nicholas had gone to France to stop him.

Further, he knew that Leclerc and the Englishman with him, Ferris, had been directly responsible for the death of Lavinia's first husband, and that Lavinia herself had been targeted by Leclerc.

But what he could not get out of his head, no matter how hard he tried, was that something had gone wrong—that someone else had been there that night. And that it was not the Frenchman, Leclerc, who had shot him in the road and left him there for dead.

"MARTINE, ARE YOU ready?" Lavinia called, tapping on the girl's door. "It is almost time to leave." Opening the door, she paused on the threshold in delight. "Oh, Martine, you look lovely! You will surely be the belle of the ball tonight.''

Martine blushed with pleasure and fingered her delicate white India-muslin gown appreciatively. ''It is lovely, *non?*''

''It and you are beautiful,'' Lavinia said, advancing into the room. ''Thank you, Hélène, you have done a marvellous job with Martine's hair.''

''Thank you, *madame*.''

''Is Nicholas here yet?'' Martine asked softly.

''Not yet, but he will be here any minute now.''

Nicholas had resolutely avoided all functions to which he received invitations, saying that he preferred quiet evenings spent with Lavinia. But this time, Martine had not allowed him to say no. She had bullied him until Lavinia feared he would either shout at her or give in. Thankfully, he had not shouted.

''Now, you must help Nicholas tonight, Martine,'' Lavinia said as they walked down the curving staircase together. ''This is not going to be easy for him.''

''Poor Nicholas. I hope he will get his memory back soon.''

''So do I,'' Lavinia said sincerely. ''So do I.''

''Are you still to be married?''

Lavinia tried to hide the pensive shimmer in her eyes. ''I do not know, Martine. Everything is still very...confused in Nicholas's mind. It would not be fair to push him into something for which he is not ready. Marriage is a very serious business.''

"But you still love him, yes?"

"Of course. I will always love him, no matter what happens,'' she admitted. "But I cannot expect the man to marry someone for whom he has no feelings, simply because of a prior arrangement."

"Then you must make him fall in love with you again,'' Martine declared with touching naiveté. "You made it happen once. You can make it happen again."

"Dear me, Martine, the things you say!'' Lavinia said, laughing.

Nicholas arrived just after eight o'clock, and Lavinia caught her breath at the sight of him. Impeccably attired in formal evening clothes, he cut a dashing figure. He may not have regained his memory, but he had certainly regained his health and his exceptional good looks. Even his eyes seemed to have found some of their old sparkle, very obvious now as he watched her approach in the gown of sapphire-blue satin.

"You look a vision, Lavinia,'' he said, bowing over her hand. "I am honoured to be escorting such a beautiful woman."

Lavinia curtsied graciously. "It is I who am

honoured by the escort of such a handsome gentleman, my lord. I vow the ladies will be watching me with envy tonight.''

''Mmm, those who are not pitying you,'' Nicholas said with a sudden return of bitterness.

Lavinia refused to allow him to sink into the depression that so coloured his moods of late. ''None of them will be pitying me, I can assure you.''

''Nicholas!''

They both turned at the sound of Martine's voice in the doorway. Immediately, Nicholas's features relaxed into an easy grin. *''Ma belle, vous êtes très jolie.''*

''Nicholas,'' Lavinia chided him.

''Hmm? Oh yes, excuse me,'' he said with a devilish grin. ''I'm not supposed to be encouraging your French, am I. Then let me say, in English, how very pretty you look. The gentlemen will be very busy vying for your regard.''

Martine sparkled under his praise. ''Thank you, Nicholas. But I already know it will be *maman* who sparkles. Does she not look beautiful?''

Nicholas levelled a smiling glance in her direction, and was about to voice his agreement, when suddenly a flash of another night edged up from his subconscious. A blue gown. The memory of

Martine's words…of his looking at Lavinia's throat, and of seeing…''

''The necklace,'' he said abruptly. ''Where is the necklace?''

''Oh, I did not think to wear…'' Lavinia gasped, her hand going to her throat even as she stared at him in shock. ''Nicholas! You remember…the necklace?''

Martine glanced at her mother with an expression of delight. ''*Oui,* the diamonds, yes. With sapphires. You remembered!''

''Yes, to match…your engagement ring,'' Nicholas said, his excitement mounting.

''Nicholas, you do remember!'' Lavinia cried. ''You remembered the necklace you bought for me! It was part of my betrothal gift!''

Nicholas felt a shudder of exhilaration. Dear God, was it possible? Was it happening at last?

''Yes, I remember,'' he said, quickly. ''I remember that…there was a necklace. That you were wearing it…with this gown the…last time.''

''At our betrothal party. Do you remember that, Nicholas?''

He tried. He tried harder than he had ever tried before. He felt both Martine and Lavinia urging him to dig back and pull the memories out of his mind.

But he couldn't. It had come like a brief flash

of lightning, and it had gone just as swiftly. He remembered the necklace, and he remembered Lavinia wearing it...but he remembered nothing beyond that.

"No, there is...nothing else," he said bitterly. "Damn! It lasted for but a moment."

Lavinia refused to allow the significance of the moment to pale. "But it was a moment, Nicholas," she whispered, holding his hand tightly in hers. "A moment that will lead to others. The important thing now is that there is room for hope. You have just proven that."

IT WAS PERHAPS because of the remarkable occurrence of his remembering the necklace that Nicholas set off for the ball in a spirit of considerable optimism. The fact that he had remembered anything—even something as inconsequential as a necklace—proved that there was indeed hope. And it was perhaps his unusual vivacity—more evident than upon any occasion since his return to London—that caused people to gravitate towards him, drawn as they had always been by his irresistible wit and charm.

"Well, Lord Longworth, I am delighted to see you in such a good mood this evening," Lady Wolverton commented with delight. "Is there a reason for this return of high spirits?"

Nicholas shook his head, having decided not to tell anyone about what had happened. "None at all, Lady Wolverton. I simply came to the realization today that there is no point in bemoaning the fact that I can remember nothing, but rather that I should be thankful that I am alive, as Lavinia keeps pointing out." He turned and glanced at his radiant fiancée with a pride he did not need to pretend. "She is a very special lady, and I am very lucky to have her."

Lady Wolverton beamed. "Does this mean that we may still be hearing wedding bells in the near future?"

"I think it is a little too early for that, Lady Wolverton," Lavinia said self-consciously. "There is still much that Lord Longworth and I need to understand. After all, it is like getting to know someone again for the first time."

"Well, if the two of you end up looking as happy as you did the first time, I shouldn't imagine the nuptials will be all that far off. I shan't soon forget that beautiful toast you gave to Lavinia at your betrothal party, Lord Longworth. I must admit, it near moved me to tears. Or perhaps this young lady will beat you both to the altar," Lady Wolverton said, smiling benevolently on Martine. "You are a most popular young lady with the gentlemen, Miss Duplesse. No doubt you will receive a number of offers before the end of the Season.''

Martine blushed in a charming fashion. ''Thank you, Lady Wolverton, but I should prefer to see *maman* settled first.''

Lady Wolverton shook her head. ''Charming, utterly charming. She is a credit to you, Lavinia. I even heard Sally Jersey remarking on her the other day. I vow it will not be long before you receive her vouchers for Almack's.''

''That would, of course, be delightful,'' Lavinia said, knowing that the all-important vouchers were mandatory for any hopeful young lady's success in Society.

''Ah, now there is a face I have not seen in a long time,'' Lady Wolverton commented suddenly, glancing over Lavinia's shoulder. ''Such a handsome man. And so very distinguished. Lord Rushton!'' she called.

Lavinia kept the smile on her face, though she could not explain the tiny shiver that coursed through her body.

''Dear me, you cannot be cold, Lavinia,'' Lady Wolverton whispered as the gentleman approached. ''It is warm enough in here to poach an egg. Ah, my dear Lord Rushton, how good of you to come. Do you know Lady Duplesse?''

Rushton bowed, his eyes lingering appreciatively on Lavinia's face. "Yes. We met at Lady Renton's musicale. Good evening, Lady Duplesse."

"Lord Rushton. May I present my fiancé, Lord Longworth."

Nicholas turned and extended his hand to the new arrival. "Rushton."

"Longworth. I understand you had something of an accident in France," Rushton said. "Feeling better now?"

"Yes, much better, thank you."

As they were speaking, another gentleman drifted over to join them. "Evening, all," he said genially.

"Lord Havermere, how delightful to see you again," Lady Wolverton gushed. "We were just talking about Lord Longworth's unfortunate accident in France."

"Dear me, yes, I heard all about it," Havermere said, clearly concerned. "What frightful business. Do you remember much of what happened, Lord Longworth?"

Nicholas shook his head. "Not a thing, I'm afraid. The doctors told me it was probably as a result of the head injury I suffered."

"Dashed nuisance. No memory at all, then?"

"None."

"Do they hold out any hope that it will come back?" Lady Wolverton enquired anxiously.

Nicholas managed to keep his frustration at bay. "Very little."

During the conversation, Rushton's attention strayed, and he now stood smiling down at Martine. "Well, well, never tell me that this beautiful young woman is Miss Martine Duplesse?"

Martine's surprise was evident. "You know me?"

"Indeed." Rushton pressed a quick kiss to the back of her hand. *"Enchanté, mademoiselle."*

Martine gasped, her eyes lighting up. *"Vous parlez français, monsieur?"*

"Martine, English please," Lavinia reminded her.

Rushton glanced in amusement at Lavinia. "Surely you do not object to your stepdaughter speaking French, Lady Duplesse? It is her native tongue, after all."

"Martine is allowed to speak French at home, Lord Rushton, but at social functions I prefer that she use English," Lavinia said calmly. "I feel it is important that she become fully conversant with the language of the country she is living in. Do you think that wrong?"

"Not at all. I have always thought it is a sign

of respect to speak the language of the country one is in. It has always stood me in good stead.''

''Do you speak other languages, Lord Rushton?'' Martine asked, intrigued.

''A few.''

Lavinia regarded him narrowly. ''You speak French like a native. Have you spent much time abroad?''

Rushton smiled obliquely. ''Not recently. As I am sure you will agree, France is very dangerous just now, and I consider myself an Englishman, first and last. But that is not to say that I do not enjoy what Paris has to offer. Just as I enjoy the pleasures of many other European cities. Venice, Rome, Florence, to name but a few.''

Martine fairly devoured him with her eyes. ''Ah, but you are so well travelled, *monsieur*. How exciting it must be to see all those places.''

''Before the war, I was able to travel freely on the Continent, visiting the other great cities. Places like Salzburg and Vienna.'' Rushton's eyes were warm as they lingered on the girl's face. ''Sadly, we are much more restricted now.''

''Vienna!'' Martine sighed rapturously. ''I should so love to go there. *La cité de la musique.*''

''The city of music,'' Havermere translated, displaying his own knowledge of the language.

''Yes, there is much music,'' Rushton said.

"Music inspired by the great composers. Perhaps one day you will see these wonderful places, Miss Duplesse."

Martine's eyes were glowing as they rested on the man's face. "*J'espère*... that is, I hope so, *monsieur*. And soon."

"Well, not too soon, perhaps," Lady Wolverton spoke up. "I am sure a number of English gentlemen would like to have the opportunity of meeting you first, my dear. Speaking of which, would you mind if I introduced Martine to Lady Trevor's son, Lavinia? He has been most anxious to meet her." Lady Wolverton leaned a little closer. "Quite taken with her already, I fancy, as are a number of them."

Lavinia carefully hid her smile. "Yes, by all means, Lady Wolverton."

To this point, Nicholas had been content to stand back and listen. But when he happened to glance towards the door and see Edward, he touched Lavinia's shoulder gently. "Lavinia, would you excuse me for a moment? I have just seen Edward come in."

Lavinia nodded. "Yes, of course. I shall find you directly."

When he was gone, Lavinia turned to find Lord Rushton watching her, the same speculative look in his eye as she had seen at Lady Renton's musicale.

"Did you wish to ask me something, Lord Rushton?" Lavinia enquired candidly, aware of Lord Havermere watching them both.

"Not at all, Lady Duplesse. I was merely thinking what a charming young lady your stepdaughter is. Is she happy living in London after growing up in France?"

"She is adjusting well."

He nodded, watching Martine across the length of the floor. "Beautiful. As her mother was."

Lavinia started. "I wasn't aware you knew Genevieve Duplesse that well."

"I knew your whole family. Or rather, your husband's."

Rushton's eyes were veiled, and it seemed to Lavinia that there was a great deal he wasn't telling her. She was just about to ask, when his next question forestalled her.

"I wonder, Lady Duplesse, if you might allow me to call upon Miss Duplesse tomorrow. I should like to take her driving in the Park."

Lavinia felt a knot form in the pit of her stomach, and hoped her alarm was not evident. "Unfortunately, my daughter and I are getting ready to go down to the country for a while, my lord. As

such, there are a great many things we have to
attend to. I'm sure you understand.''

Rushton bowed graciously. If he had detected
the slight note of reserve in her voice, he gave no
sign. ''But of course. Perhaps I may call upon her
when you return.''

''If that is to her liking,'' Lavinia told him carefully.

''Your servant, *madame*.''

''Lady Duplesse,'' Havermere said, moving off
with Rushton.

Not until the two men were well away did Lavinia let out the breath she had unconsciously been
holding. Hearing Martine's approach, she was
careful to greet her with a bright smile. ''Are you
having a good time, my dear?''

''*Oui,* a very good time, *maman*.'' Martine
glanced shyly at Rushton's retreating back. ''Lord
Rushton is a most handsome gentleman, is he not?
And so distinguished.''

Lavinia's smile was forced. ''Yes, but then, he
is a lot older than you, Martine. In fact, he is almost your father's age. But now, what did you
think of Lady Trevor's son?''

Martine nodded, though with a definite lack of
enthusiasm. ''He is a nice boy.''

Lavinia did not miss the implication. ''He may
be a boy, Martine, but rather a boy than a man

jaded by life,'' she murmured, more to herself than to her stepdaughter.

Unfortunately, Martine heard. "Lord Rushton did not sound jaded to me. In fact, I found him very interesting indeed. And so handsome, yes?''

Lavinia did not reply. Yes, Lord Rushton was handsome. Too handsome. His were the type of looks that caused impressionable young women to do foolish things. Still, if it were only his looks that disturbed her, Lavinia would not have minded nearly so much.

ACROSS THE ROOM, Nicholas sipped his champagne and glanced out over the jostling crowd. "Do you know, Edward, it is amazing. All these people, and no more than ten to whom I could put a name. And then only with Lavinia's assistance.''

Edward gave his friend a lopsided grin. "Count yourself fortunate, Nicholas. I myself would be happy to recognize so few.''

Nicholas glanced at him shrewdly. "Not a lover of these affairs, eh?''

Edward shrugged. "Not particularly. Still, it's all part of the game, I suppose, but one, I admit, I've never found much time for.'' His own eyes darkened. "What I saw during my time in France made all this appear very frivolous to me. I only went back into Society for my sister's sake. And for Laura's, of course.''

''Your sister Charlotte?'' Nicholas said, recalling what Lavinia had told him.

''Yes. She is now married to the Earl of Marwood. Splendid fellow. But then, you knew him well.''

Nicholas blinked. ''I did?''

''One of your closest friends. You stood up for him at his wedding.''

''Did I, by Jove? And how did I come to know you?''

''Osborne sent you to France to help me escape.''

''Dear me, what an exciting life I've led,'' Nicholas commented sardonically. ''What I wouldn't give to remember it all.'' Glancing about the room, Nicholas noticed Havermere and Rushton still standing beside Lavinia. ''Edward, do you know those two gentlemen talking to Lavinia?''

Edward peered across the room. ''Rushton and Havermere, you mean?''

''Yes. What do you know about them?''

''Not a great deal. Havermere has an estate up in Scotland, where I believe he spends most of the year. As for Rushton, he keeps pretty much to himself.''

''Are they good friends?''

"They seem to be. They're often at each other's estates. Apparently, they've been in Scotland for the past month. I hear the salmon fishing is very good."

"What about Rushton?" Nicholas asked. "Is he married?"

"No. Seems to like the ladies well enough, but never bothers with any particular one for any length of time. Havermere is definitely more the lady's man. He's kept a string of mistresses in Kensington. Why?"

"I don't know. There's just something about Rushton that bothers me. Damned if I know what it is, though."

Edward glanced at the man again. "Can't recall having heard any unsavoury rumours about him. He used to spend a lot of time in France, though he's kept a pretty low profile these last few years. I believe his mother was a French aristocrat. His father was, of course, English."

"And Havermere?"

"Bit of a dandy, I suppose, but an affable-enough fellow. Born in London, spent part of his childhood in France, I believe, and travelled extensively with his tutor."

Nicholas watched the two for a moment, his eyes going back to Rushton. The man's manners were impeccable. He was attentive to a fault. Nicholas's gaze narrowed as he saw Rushton's eyes linger on Martine. ''I don't like the way he's looking at Martine.''

''I shouldn't worry about it,'' Edward replied casually. ''Probably just wishing he were a good deal younger. Lavinia's stepdaughter is a devilishly pretty girl.''

''Who is a devilishly pretty girl, Edward?'' Laura asked with a hint of amusement in her voice.

''No one you need worry about, my love. I was just telling Nicholas that Martine Duplesse is a diamond.''

''Oh, yes, I agree with you there,'' Laura said with a charming laugh. ''And such a sweet thing. I overheard some of the tabbies talking amongst themselves earlier. It would appear they are most upset with her.''

''They are?'' Nicholas frowned. ''But why?''

''It seems that they want very much to dislike her, but are finding it exceedingly difficult to do so.''

Nicholas laughed, and suddenly felt as though a weight had been lifted from his shoulders. Perhaps it wouldn't turn out so badly after all, he reflected stoically. Lord Osborne had told him that he had accomplished in France what he had set out to do. Lavinia was still in love with him, Martine was cutting a dash in Society and he was beginning to feel at home again in the glittering world that was London. Would it not be simpler just to give in and enjoy what he had?

It would, if it were not for this damned nagging suspicion that something had gone dreadfully wrong in France.

CHAPTER SEVEN

THE DAY BEFORE they set off for the country, an
event took place that caused Lavinia considerable
distress and which lingered in her mind for some
time after. She and Laura had spent the better part
of the morning idly browsing through the shops
for some last-minute purchases. Martine had not
accompanied them, saying that she wished to remain at home to write some letters. But when Lavinia and Laura returned, it was to learn that Martine was not at home, and that a gentleman had
called and taken her driving. Lavinia paused in the
act of removing her gloves. "Which gentleman,
Habinger?"

"Lord Rushton, my lady."

"Rushton!"

The note of annoyance in her voice was unmistakable, and Laura glanced at her in surprise. "Is
there something wrong with Lord Rushton, Lavinia?"

"Wrong? No, not exactly," she said quickly,
still unable to pinpoint what it was about Rushton

that disturbed her. "It is just that I am not...
pleased by his attentions towards Martine. The
man is old enough to be her father."

Laura shrugged gracefully. "I am sure it is
naught but a passing fancy, Lavinia. You said
yourself that Martine is interested in travelling.
Perhaps it is Lord Rushton's knowledge of other
cities she finds fascinating."

Recalling the look in Martine's eyes the evening
she and Lord Rushton had met, however, Lavinia
wasn't so sure. There was something about the
older man that fascinated her stepdaughter, and
whether it was indeed his sophistication, or the air
of mystery that surrounded him, Lavinia knew that
his impression upon Martine had been a strong
one.

She was suddenly very glad that they would be
leaving for Rose Cottage on the morrow. Perhaps
the journey by carriage would provide a good opportunity for the two of them to have a mother-
daughter chat. She also decided to speak to Lord
Rushton when he and Martine returned.

"When are you and Edward coming down?"
Lavinia asked, changing the subject as they moved
into the parlour.

"Well, to be perfectly honest," Laura replied,
"Edward thought we should give you and Nicholas
some time alone together."

Lavinia saw her friend's cheeks colour and she laughed. "Laura, it is very good of you, but it is really not necessary. Besides, Nicholas and I will hardly be alone, what with Martine and a full retinue of servants travelling down with us."

"No, but you know what I mean," Laura said, her eyes twinkling. "In answer to your question, however, I shall probably arrive on Thursday, and I believe Edward is planning to follow on the Saturday."

"Good. Then I shall arrange some entertainments for the weekend," Lavinia said brightly. "There are some people in the area I like very much and have not seen these last few years. It will be a good excuse to have them to visit." She glanced at Laura warmly. "I should not like you and Edward to be bored while you are with us."

"Nonsense! How could I possibly be bored?" Laura said quickly. "After these last few months I should be quite happy to escape to the peace and quiet of the country for a while. It will also give me time to prepare for our wedding."

Lavinia glanced at her, unable to prevent a fleeting touch of envy. "Are you excited?"

"Dreadfully! I cannot wait to be married to Edward." Laura slid a shy glance towards Lavinia. "Is that…terribly bold of me to say?"

"Gracious, not in the least," Lavinia assured

her. "I should far rather hear you say that you were excited about the wedding than apprehensive about it."

Laura's pretty face clouded momentarily. "Will it trouble you, Lavinia, coming to our wedding?"

She knew what her friend was referring to, and shook her head. "No. While Nicholas and I have been forced to delay our own wedding, it does not mean I would resent going to yours. But you are a dear for asking. I hope very much that ours will still take place."

"Do you think some time in the country will help him?"

"I do hope so," Lavinia admitted. "Nicholas has been under so much strain since his return. He's pushing himself to remember, and when he doesn't, I fear it only increases the pressure that much more. I am hoping that in the country he will be able to forget about what happened. He's never met the people I will be introducing him to, so he won't have to force himself to try to remember them."

Just then, Lavinia heard the sound of the front door opening, followed by Martine's pretty laughter. She rose and went out immediately. Lord Rushton was standing in the hall just behind the girl.

"Oh, *maman!* We had such a lovely time!"

Martine's eyes were shining. "Lord Rushton has been telling me the most wonderful stories of his travels. I almost felt as though I were there myself."

Lavinia forced a pleasant smile to her lips, even though her heart was sinking. Her stepdaughter's face was positively glowing.

"Run along upstairs and change, my dear. Your tea will be ready soon."

Martine's smile faded a little at the unexpected sharpness in her mother's voice. *"Oui, maman."* She turned towards the gentleman standing silently behind them. *"Merci, monsieur.* I enjoyed the drive very much."

Rushton bowed gallantly. "It was my pleasure, Miss Duplesse. I look forward to having the opportunity again."

With another quick glance at Lavinia, Martine ran lightly up the stairs. When she had gone, Lavinia turned back towards Lord Rushton, her own smile disappearing. "I would prefer in future, Lord Rushton, that you ask my permission before taking my stepdaughter out."

Rushton eyed her speculatively. "Your daughter is no longer a schoolroom miss, Lady Duplesse. She is of an age to receive visits from gentlemen."

"I did not say that she was not," Lavinia said quietly. "But she is still very new to English ways and I will not allow her to entertain or be entertained, by gentlemen without my knowledge.''

"I can assure you, Lady Duplesse, my intentions were strictly honourable. In fact, it was a rather spur-of-the-moment idea on my part. When I realized that you were leaving for the country soon, I merely thought that most of your arrangements would have been taken care of and that Miss Duplesse might have some time on her hands." He smiled in a charming fashion. "She did not seem unhappy to see me."

"Still, I would have preferred that you ask me first, Lord Rushton. Martine is young and impressionable. She is not in the least sophisticated, and I will not see her hurt. Do I make myself clear?''

Rushton regarded the woman in front of him with an expression akin to amusement. Her anger had heightened the colour in her cheeks and caused her eyes to flash with azure fire. She was an incredibly beautiful woman, and Rushton wondered that he had never noticed it before. She was like a lioness protecting her cub. Still, he was also aware that in the jungle, only the fittest survived.

He bowed mockingly. "Quite clear, Lady Duplesse. I take it you are warning me to stay away from her?"

"I think it might be better, my lord," Lavinia agreed quietly. "I hardly need point out that you are considerably older than my stepdaughter. No doubt you would soon grow tired of her youthful ways.''

''On the contrary, I find the young lady's naiveté refreshing. However, I will endeavour to respect your wishes. Although perhaps it is Miss Duplesse you should be speaking with, rather than myself.''

Lavinia did not care for the insinuation, but understood him well enough. ''I shall speak with my stepdaughter, Lord Rushton. Of that you may be sure.''

Rushton bowed again, a faintly contemptuous glitter in his eye. ''Young ladies can be powerfully stubborn when they want to be.''

''Good day, Lord Rushton!''

Her anger seemed to have no effect on him whatsoever, and he turned to leave with that same mocking smile hovering about his lips. After the door closed, Lavinia clenched her hands into fists.

She had made an enemy today. And the fact that it was a man she had not been able to trust from the moment she'd met him did nothing in the least to allay her fears.

She would watch Martine very carefully from now on.

ROSE COTTAGE was a beautiful country house of graceful proportions and comfortable size. A fifteenth-century manor house with additions made early in the seventeenth century, it had drawn its name from the magnificent rose gardens that surrounded it. The house had long been in Lavinia's family, and yet it was the one place she had never shown François. He had expressed no desire to explore the English countryside, preferring to return to France as soon as possible after their wedding.

Looking back now, Lavinia was relieved. The house held no unpleasant memories for her. It was as calming and as restful as it had always been. Happily, Nicholas felt its tranquillity at once.

"It is so peaceful here," he murmured as Lavinia led him down one of the many intimate walks that wound through the extensive gardens. "A man could be completely at rest here."

Lavinia smiled and tucked her arm into his. "I certainly hope so, Nicholas. That was my reason for wanting to bring you."

Nicholas turned and looked into her face. "Was I so admirable a man that I inspired this kind of devotion in you, Lavinia?"

Her smile was as gentle as a mother's toward a newborn babe. "There has never been anyone like you in my life, Nicholas. Even without your memory, you are still the man I fell in love with. Your character has not changed, only your knowledge of the past. You are as good and as loving as you always were.''

He stared down into her eyes. ''I want so much to remember, Lavinia,'' he whispered desperately. ''I want to feel again, to live and breathe as the man I was. I want to remember how much I loved you.''

''And I truly hope you will, my darling,'' Lavinia replied huskily, moved as always by his nearness. ''We can stay here for as long as you wish.''

Nicholas laughed throatily. ''Are you not afraid of being branded a loose woman, Lavinia Duplesse?'' he teased her. ''There are those who will comment upon our staying so long together in the country.''

''Let them say what they will,'' she replied calmly. ''I am doing nothing wrong. We are suitably chaperoned by my stepdaughter and the servants, and Edward and Laura will be joining us shortly, as well as other guests.''

''Other guests?'' Nicholas looked wary. ''You did not tell me anyone else would be coming from London.''

''No, not from London,'' Lavinia assured him. ''These are friends of mine who live in the area. Friends I have not seen in a long time.''

''Will they not be…surprised to find you here with me?'' Nicholas asked.

"No. They did not know François, though they heard of his death." Lavinia's voice was matter-of-fact. "And they knew that I was to be married again. They will know soon enough that you have had an accident, if they have not already heard."

Momentarily, a look of unhappiness settled on Nicholas's handsome features. "Yes, is there anyone who does not know that Viscount Longworth is starting all over again—that his memory was wiped clean by a stray bullet?"

Lavinia heard the bitterness in his voice, and her heart went out to him. "Oh, Nicholas, you must put the anger aside. You are alive, my darling, and that is all that matters. And there is hope. Or have you forgotten the necklace?"

At the mention of his one brief moment of lucidity, Nicholas sighed. "No, I have not forgotten. I cling to it like a drowning man to a raft. But the knowledge that there have been no more such occurrences frightens me." He grasped her hands with feverish intensity. "I tried so hard to hold on to that moment, Lavinia—to see beyond the necklace, to remember something else that had happened that night, anything at all. But there was nothing."

"Of course not, because you were trying too hard," Lavinia chastised him. "The memory of the necklace came to you when you were not even thinking of it. That is how it will happen, Nicholas, I feel sure of it,'' she said earnestly as they began to walk again. ''When you least expect it, something will come into your mind. That is why I wanted you to come here with me. Here,'' she said, glancing around at the beautiful surroundings, ''all is peace and tranquillity. Here, there are no memories for you to struggle with. Here, your mind will be clear.''

Nicholas abruptly halted and drew Lavinia into the circle of his arms. ''And here, there is no one to disturb my time with you.''

His voice, deep and sensual, sent a shiver of desire through her. ''There is Martine,'' she reminded him softly.

''Mmm.'' He nuzzled his lips gently against her cheek. ''Dear Martine, who would very much like to see me fall in love with her mother again.''

Lavinia blushed, but did not bother denying what they both knew to be the truth. She glanced up at him, doubt and concern reflected in her eyes. ''Oh, Nicholas, it is the dearest wish of my heart that you could. But if it does not happen, I will not hold you. You are free to go at any time. You know that, don't you?'' she whispered.

Nicholas looked down into her eyes and saw no duplicity there. She meant every word she said.

She was willing to let him go altogether, rather than have him stay out of a sense of obligation.

"I know, Lavinia," he breathed softly. "And you may rest assured that, if I stay, it will be only for the right reasons. But I would be lying if I did not tell you that I already feel myself extremely drawn to you."

Lavinia strove for a bantering tone, which was very difficult, given the tempting proximity of his lips. "You are drawn to me because you have not been exposed to any other attractive ladies. I wonder if you would not choose a younger lady, were you to be given the choice."

Nicholas laughed. "They would have to be very special young ladies indeed to compare to you. The more time I spend with you, the more I am convinced that you are truly a remarkable woman...."

His lips met hers, and Lavinia groaned softly as she willingly returned his kiss. Lifting her arms, she twined her fingers in his dark curls. Her heart soared as he pulled her closer against his firm body, moulding her to him. In that one kiss she communicated everything to him: her love, her longing, her need.

Yes, her need. A need that urged him to reach up and tentatively touch the aching fullness of her breasts through the silkiness of her gown. A need that inspired her gasp of pleasure as his thumb caresses grew more impassioned.

But it was a need that would never be fully satisfied in the garden of her home, Lavinia realized tremulously. Hopefully, there would come a time when the two of them could be together, but this was not it. She drew back out of his arms, even as he went to unfasten her bodice.

"Lavinia...." His voice was rough with desire. They were both breathing unsteadily.

"No, Nicholas, I cannot. Not now. Not like this..."

Her voice throbbed with suppressed emotion, and suddenly, Nicholas knew how hard this was for her. She was drawing on reserves far deeper than his.

He hung his head in shame, dropping his hands. "Forgive me, Lavinia, I...don't know what came over me. I should never have done that."

Summoning a shaky smile, she pressed her finger against his lips, silencing him. "No, my darling, do not apologize. I wanted it as much as you. More, perhaps," she admitted huskily, knowing how badly she had wanted him to go on touching her. "But perhaps it is better that we...take our time. I would not want you to think...ill of me."

Nicholas shook his head fiercely. "I could never think ill of you. And I would never doubt that anything which happened between us could happen for any but the right reasons.''

Lavinia laughed shakily. "Nevertheless, we are still, for all intents and purposes, a betrothed couple, Lord Longworth," she said with mock primness. "And it would not do to allow our emotions to sweep us headlong down a path from which there could be no return.''

Nicholas laughed, and the tension eased. "Dear me, Lady Duplesse, such philosophical thoughts. I never dreamed you to be so profound.''

"Oh, I assure you, there are many things you do not know about me, Lord Longworth." She smiled as they turned back towards the house. "Not yet, at any rate.''

THE FIRST THREE DAYS at Rose Cottage were delightful in their simplicity. Lavinia spent as much time in Nicholas's company as he seemed to want, and divided the rest of her hours between Martine and her other pastimes. Thankfully, her stepdaughter, who had displayed an uncustomary stiffness with Lavinia after the incident with Lord Rushton, soon regained her normal *joie de vivre* and began enjoying her holiday in the English countryside.

The three of them rode together every day, setting out from the stables just after breakfast and sometimes not returning until early afternoon. Lavinia had the cook prepare a hamper of food for the groom to carry. When they came upon a particularly lovely vista, the groom would simply unfurl the blanket, set out the plates and cutlery and unpack the simple, yet delicious meal Cook had provided.

As the days passed, Lavinia was delighted to see the last remaining traces of anxiety pass from Nicholas's face. He laughed frequently, and Lavinia often caught his eyes on her when she turned to look at him.

Even Martine noticed his increased attention. "I think Nicholas is falling in love with you, *maman*," she said one afternoon as the two of them sat in companionable silence in the conservatory. "He follows you with his eyes."

Lavinia tried not to show how happy that made her. "I hope you are right, Martine, but it is still early yet."

"He is looking better though, *non?*"

"Yes, much better. I think Rose Cottage agrees with him."

Martine smiled secretly. "I think it is *l'amour* that agrees with him."

Lavinia blushed and returned her attention to her book. But the pages of her novel did not hold her attention. It was true, she and Nicholas did seem to be growing closer. He always had a gentle smile

for her, a tender word. And lately, his kisses had
been growing more impassioned, reminding her of
the way he had kissed her just before he had gone
to France.

Oh, dear God, let it be as it was, Lavinia prayed
silently. *Bring him back to me just the way he was.*

NICHOLAS SAT WITH his hands resting on the pom-
mel of his saddle and gazed down at Rose Cottage,
aware of an undeniable feeling of contentment. A
thin plume of smoke rose from one of the largest
chimneys, and he could imagine Lavinia curled up
in front of the fire with a novel. Martine was probably beside her, lost in the pages of her own book,
looking for all the world like a kitten curled up
cosily beside her mother.

Nicholas sighed. Did he have a place in that picture? At times he thought he did. When he was
with Lavinia, everything felt so right. But when he
was away from her, the doubts came crowding in.
Who was he? What had happened in his life to this
point? And what had happened that night in France
that had changed the course of his destiny?

Suddenly, the anger that always accompanied
such thoughts surrounded Nicholas, obliterating his
happiness and plunging him into gloom. Though
he had been less inclined to suffer these fits of

depression since coming to Rose Cottage, he had still not been able to escape them altogether.

Why could he not accept that it was Leclerc who had shot him that night? Why did he keep thinking that there was more? What else could have happened?

Nicholas groaned in frustration. Lavinia was right. The harder he tried to remember, the more the truth eluded him. Sometimes at night he felt vague stirrings of memory coming back to haunt him. He caught glimpses of the man he had been, faces of people he'd known—elusive, dancing shadows that hovered on the very brink of his awareness. But as soon as he tried to reach out and touch them, they disappeared like moonbeams in the first light of dawn.

But at least they came, Nicholas told himself. He'd have to be content with that. And most of the time he was, always knowing that tomorrow was another day, and possibly one day closer to recovery.

CONTRARY TO LAURA'S original plans, she and Edward arrived together on the Friday. Waving aside their apologies for the last-minute change, Lavinia had the butler deal with the luggage and then happily welcomed her guests.

"Lavinia, your house is simply breathtaking," Laura exclaimed, sighing enviously as they toured the main floor. "How can you bear to be away from it?"

"The time I spend away from it makes me appreciate it all the more when I am here," Lavinia explained simply. "Come, let us retire to the drawing-room. From there, you have the view onto the rose gardens."

Martine joined them just as tea was being served. "Good afternoon, Mademoiselle Beaufort, Monsieur Kingsley."

"Good day, Martine. Are you enjoying your holiday at Rose Cottage?" Edward enquired.

"Ah, oui, c'est très—," The girl broke off, seeing Lavinia's raised eyebrow, then continued with enthusiasm, "It is very beautiful. Has *maman* told you about the *soirée* yet?"

Laura glanced at her hostess. "No, she hasn't. Have you planned it then, Lavinia?"

"Yes. I have already sent out invitations and everyone has accepted."

"Oh, how marvellous. It will be like old times, will it not, Edward?"

"Yes, or rather, almost," he said. His gaze slid to Nicholas, who had been sitting quietly, listening to the ladies chat. "Any improvement, my friend?"

Nicholas flushed, but then, realizing he was with his closest friends, he let his features relax. "No,

I'm afraid not. I sometimes catch brief glimpses of people or places, but nothing stays with me.''

''Still, there was the incident with the necklace,'' Laura reminded him. ''That was very positive.''

Nicholas nodded. He had agreed to let Lavinia tell Edward and Laura about the breakthrough, but no one else. ''Yes. Unfortunately, there hasn't been a reoccurrence. I keep hoping, of course.''

''Never mind,'' Edward said in a tone of encouragement. ''It has not been all that long since the accident, and the doctors did say that if your memory were to return, it might not be for a while.''

''Yes, I know. It's just that I find myself growing anxious for it to happen. Was I always so impatient?''

''Always! Impatient and stubborn,'' Edward told him, laughing.

''Dear me, what an unlovable cad,'' Nicholas replied with a mock frown. ''Can't think why anyone would be in a hurry to have the old Nicholas back.''

''I can.''

His gaze swivelled round to Lavinia's, and he saw the answer reflected in her eyes. ''Apart from you, that is, my dear,'' he amended softly.

Lavinia smiled, and quickly turned her attention to the refreshments. Perhaps God had heard her prayer after all.

CHAPTER EIGHT

"*MAMAN*, MAY I go into town?" Martine asked Lavinia the following afternoon. "I should like to get some new ribbon for my bonnet."

Lavinia nodded. "Yes, of course, Martine. One of the grooms can drive you."

"Oh, that's all right," the girl said quickly. "I can drive the curricle myself. Nicholas has been teaching me."

"Has he indeed?" Lavinia slid an amused glance towards Laura, who was sitting in a winged-back chair doing needlework. "Well, in that case, I suppose it would be all right. But take Hélène with you."

"Yes, *maman*."

"And do not be late."

"No, *maman*."

As Martine scurried out, Laura shook her head. "Dear me, that girl is so full of life. Does she not wear you out?"

"At times," Lavinia admitted. "She forgets to behave like a properly reared young lady sometimes, but I tend to let her get away with it. I was inclined to such boisterousness in my own youth. Besides, she was such a serious girl when I met her. François did not approve of frivolity in young ladies.''

''Well, she has certainly blossomed under your care. Has there been any further mention of Lord Rushton?''

''No, thank goodness!'' Lavinia replied. ''And I have not brought the subject up. I may be an ostrich sticking my head in the sand, but I should rather like to think that out of sight is out of mind. Besides, I did ask Lord Rushton to stay away from her, and I hope he is gentleman enough to comply.''

''Well, as you say, Lavinia, Martine is an impressionable girl. No doubt her head will be turned many times before she meets the young man who will finally capture her heart as well as her head.''

''I hope so.'' A frown marred the smooth line of Lavinia's forehead. ''Martine has always been so intense, so…passionate in her approach to life. When she takes to something, it becomes the centre of her world—for as long as it remains with her. Then it is discarded, as another new passion moves in to take its place.'' She levelled a meaningful glance at Laura. ''I can only hope it is that way with Lord Rushton.''

"You think she is infatuated with him?"

Lavinia nodded, her eyes troubled. "Yes, I do. I can tell you, Laura, I was very glad we left for the country when we did. As far as I am concerned, the less Martine sees of that man, the better!"

THE GUESTS LAVINIA HAD invited for dinner that evening were a delightful couple, and Nicholas warmed to them immediately. Anthony Hewitt, a tall, solidly built man close in age to Nicholas and Edward, was as well informed on sports and current affairs as any London gentleman. He travelled to Town frequently, but he preferred the comfort of his large country property in Kent.

His wife Pamela, on the other hand, was a soft-spoken young woman who looked hardly old enough to be the mother of two healthy children and the mistress of such a sprawling estate. She watched her husband with pride, and it was clear that a mutual bond of love and affection bound them together. Dinner was a light-hearted affair, punctuated with much laughter and many shared remembrances of earlier days.

"Oh, yes, Lavinia was a dreadful child," Anthony Hewitt confided as the dinner plates were being cleared away. "Pushed me into the lake once, then took off like a frightened colt. I didn't see her again for days."

"Do you blame me?" Lavinia retaliated. "I saw you waiting for me down by the gate, Anthony Hewitt, and I knew what you were going to do. I purposely stayed in the house."

Nicholas looked at his fiancée with an expression of amazement. "Lavinia, I would never have imagined you doing such a thing. Why on earth did you push Anthony into the lake in the first place?"

"Because he teased me," Lavinia replied. "And because he called me names."

"Anthony, you didn't!" Pamela Hewitt gasped.

"I certainly did," her husband replied without a trace of remorse. "I used to call her Misfit, because she was forever getting into scrapes. Scrapes for which *I* was always blamed."

"Aha, now the truth comes out," Pamela said. "I knew you would be involved somehow."

"I was not in the least involved," Anthony protested. "It wasn't my fault that Lavinia fell off her horse when she tried to jump bareback over the gate."

"It certainly was!" Lavinia replied, laughing. "*You* were the one who dared me to do it in the first place!"

Amidst the laughter that ensued, Lavinia did not at first notice that Martine was unusually quiet, nor that her attention seemed to be far away. But later, when the ladies retired, leaving the gentlemen to their port and cigars, she drew her stepdaughter aside. "Martine, are you feeling all right? You were very quiet during the meal."

"Yes, *maman,* I am fine. I am just a little tired," she replied diffidently

"Are you sure?" Lavinia studied the girl's face intently. "You're looking a little flushed. Not coming down with something, are you?"

"No, *maman.*"

"Well, if you're sure," Lavinia said hesitantly. "By the way, I did not see you when you came in this afternoon. You were gone quite a while. Did you find your ribbon?"

She was surprised to see the girl's cheeks grow pink. "Yes. And then I...went to the baker's and...had a biscuit."

"A biscuit. So that's why you didn't eat very much at dinner," Lavinia said, suddenly realizing why the girl had blushed; obviously, she had not intended to tell her about the treat she'd indulged in.

"I know I should not have, but I was...hungry." Martine glanced at Lavinia intently. "You're not angry, are you?"

"No, of course not," Lavinia said, surprised at the girl's apprehension. "Good heavens, if you cannot indulge yourself with a treat once in a while, what fun would there be in going out?''

Martine's expression noticeably relaxed. ''Thank you, *maman*.''

''Are you going to join us for tea?''

''If it is all right with you, I would rather…go up to my room.''

Lavinia smiled. Obviously, all the fresh air she'd had was wearing her stepdaughter out. ''Of course. Off you go then. I shall see you in the morning. Don't forget, we are going to see the cathedral tomorrow.''

''No, I had not forgotten. Good night.''

''Good night, Martine.''

Lavinia watched the girl climb the stairs and then turned to rejoin her guests, blissfully unaware of the storm that was brewing under her very nose.

LONG AFTER THE HEWITTS left and Edward and Laura retired to their respective rooms, Lavinia found herself propped up in bed, flipping through the pages of a magazine. She was not in the least tired, nor had she been for the last few nights. Given that her days were filled with activities, and her evenings with entertaining, she should have fallen into bed every night quite exhausted. And yet, again tonight, she was too restless to settle down.

The moon shining in through her window beckoned to her, and tossing aside the magazine, Lavinia rose. Slipping a robe over her nightgown, she quietly opened the door and made her way downstairs to the conservatory. Once there, she opened the door and stepped out into the night air. It was cool, but not unpleasantly so. The moon lit a brilliant path through the night, illuminating the flagstone walk as clearly as though it were day.

"You couldn't sleep either, I see."

The voice startled her, and Lavinia jumped at the sight of a shadowy figure seated on the bench ahead of her. "Nicholas! What are you doing out here so late?"

He rose as she approached, his voice a throaty whisper. "I might ask you the same thing. This is hardly the recommended strolling hour."

Lavinia chuckled, pulling her robe closely about her. She was well aware that the nearly transparent muslin did little to hide the contours of her figure.

Nicholas noticed her action. "Are you cold?"

She shook her head. She had begun to shiver but not as a result of the cold. "No."

"You are not frightened of me, I hope."

Lavinia laughed, the sound as soft as raindrops falling on a leaf. "Not in the way you might be thinking, my lord, though I confess I am very... aware of you."

Nicholas chuckled. "Yes, no doubt as much as I am aware of you in that flimsy night covering. Do you always walk about dressed so provocatively, Lady Duplesse?" he teased.

Lavinia was thankful for the darkness that hid her blush. "Odious creature, of course not. At least, not when there are gentlemen about. I simply felt the need for…a walk. A bit of air." Her brows drew together. "I found I was not the least bit sleepy tonight."

She heard Nicholas sigh. "No, I fear sleep did not come easily to me, either. Perhaps it was the wine."

"Yes, perhaps."

"Shall we walk?"

Lavinia nodded and fell into step beside him. "What did you think of the Hewitts?"

"I think that if all your friends are as charming as they, I shall never want to leave Kent," Nicholas replied with eloquent simplicity. "They made me feel most welcome this evening."

"They were comfortable with you."

"How did you know?"

"Because Anthony was more gregarious than usual. He would never have related all those childhood pranks if he didn't like you."

Nicholas suddenly started to laugh. "I admit, it

conjured up some interesting pictures. Did you really push him into the pond?"

"I most certainly did," Lavinia replied. "He made me so angry, I couldn't help myself. But I ran as fast as my legs would carry me once I realized what I'd done."

"Dearest Lavinia, I can just imagine what you looked like, running like the wind with your hair flying out behind you. Or did you wear it in braids?"

"Oh, no, it was loose most of the time," Lavinia admitted. "I could never sit still long enough for Nanny to braid it. She often told my mother I was quite hopeless."

Nicholas reached for her hand and drew her towards him. "Did she? And what would she say about you now, I wonder?"

Lavinia felt the warmth emanating from his body as he pulled her closer. "I cannot imagine that she would think me all that improved. I am quite shamelessly compromising myself by being out here all alone with you."

"Yes, you are. *And* with a man who has no memory of you," Nicholas reminded her.

Lavinia tilted her head back and gazed into his eyes. "He may have no memory of me from the past, but has he no thoughts of me in the present?"

Nicholas looked at her with an expression akin

to wonder. "You are in my thoughts constantly. In fact, I'm surprised that there is room for anything else. I wake thinking of you, I go to sleep thinking of you, and when we are together like this, I am filled with a sense of peace that pushes away all the uncertainties, all the pain. Without you, I feel as though I am only…half a man. You are part of me, Lavinia, and that frightens me."

"Frightens you?" Lavinia searched his face. "But why, my darling? Why would that frighten you?"

His burning eyes held her still. "Because if I were to lose you now, if you were suddenly to grow tired and leave me, I think I would be far worse off than a man without a memory. I would be a man…without a heart."

Lavinia felt a shudder run through her body at the intensity of his words. "I am not going to leave you, Nicholas. I will *never* leave you, even if you never regain your memory. I will love you just the way you are!"

"Lavinia!" He bent his head to kiss her—and then abruptly froze.

Lavinia felt him tense. "Nicholas, what's wrong?"

He didn't answer. He only stood, staring into space with a burning, faraway look in his eyes.

"Nicholas!" Lavinia shook him gently. "Nicholas, answer me, please! What is wrong?"

It seemed an eternity before he whispered, "There was…another man."

She gasped, feeling a shiver of fear. "Oh, my God!"

"An image of him just…appeared…in my mind," Nicholas said haltingly. "A man. An Englishman."

Lavinia struggled to understand. "You mean a man other than Ferris?"

"There were…three men." Nicholas set her gently away from him, his face twisted in concentration. "I can see them. Leclerc, Ferris and… another man who came later. A man on…horseback."

"Did he shoot Leclerc?"

Nicholas hesitated. "No. I shot Leclerc. But the other man…shot Ferris." He glanced at her in astonishment. "And then…he shot me!"

Lavinia blanched. "Dear God! But why, Nicholas? Who was he?"

"I don't know. Damn, I can't remember…what he looked like." Nicholas pressed his hands to his temples. "I just remember him being on a horse. He came out of the darkness. I remember hearing…the sound of his pistol, just before I felt the pain in my side."

"His voice, Nicholas—do you remember if he said anything to you?"

Nicholas struggled to recapture the memory, but just as with the necklace, this, too, was a brief flash and then gone. "No. That's all. Damn it! I can't remember anything else."

Lavinia felt her legs begin to tremble. "I think I would...like to sit down," she said quietly.

As if recalled from a dream, Nicholas quickly nodded. "Yes, of course. Forgive me, Lavinia. I've frightened you." He took her arm and led her to the bench. "I should not have said anything."

"No, it is better that you did," she insisted, grateful for the cool stone seat beneath her. "But it frightens me, Nicholas. Who was this man? Why did he shoot you?"

He shook his head. "I don't know. He might have been a thief, I suppose," he said, recalling how the papers had described the accident as an attempted robbery.

"Nicholas, I am frightened," Lavinia said. "What if...it wasn't a robbery? What if he was trying to..."

She couldn't finish, couldn't bring herself to say the dreadful words. Slowly, her tears began to fall. Nicholas didn't speak, either. He merely sat down on the bench beside her and pulled her into his arms, holding her tightly until she stopped crying.

But even as he did, he was painfully aware of one thing.

His feeling that something had gone wrong was not incorrect. There *had* been another man on that lonely stretch of road that night—someone who had stalked him and waited until the moment was right to shoot him down. Someone who had thought him dead and had left him that way.

Someone who was very much alive and was no doubt looking for him again!

NICHOLAS DID NOT GO back to bed that night. The memory of what he had seen banished all thought of sleep. Like a child waking to a new day, he felt as though he were on the verge of a tremendous discovery, and though his memory had not returned, he was aware of having discovered a new purpose in life. And the first person he sought to tell was Edward. He found him in the breakfast-room, enjoying a quiet cup of coffee.

''Nicholas, good morning,'' Edward greeted him. ''I thought I was the only one who rose at this ridiculous hour.''

''You might be any other morning, but not today, my friend. I did not sleep all night.'' Nicholas sat down in the chair beside him. ''Edward, I remembered something. Something terribly important.''

Edward hesitated in the act of lifting the cup to his lips. The tension in Nicholas's voice was palpable. "What?"

"There was another man on the road that night. A stranger shot Ferris—and then shot me."

"Bloody hell!" Edward put down his cup with such a bang it was amazing the fine china did not shatter. "Are you sure?"

"As sure as I can be. It came to me clearly, and completely without warning."

"Do you remember who it was? Was it someone you knew?"

Nicholas shook his head. "That's the frustrating part. I can't remember anything beyond that. I know that I had my pistol trained on Leclerc and Ferris when I heard the sound of a shot and saw Ferris go down. I remember seeing Leclerc pull a small pistol out of his pocket and aim it at me."

"Then it was Leclerc who shot you."

"No. I fired first. I know I hit him. And he told me—" Nicholas broke off, his face twisting "—he told me he was…not really Leclerc. But before I had a chance to ask him what he meant, he died. That's when I heard the sound of a pistol cocking, and then a bullet hit me in the side."

Edward searched his friend's grim face. "You know what this means, don't you?"

Nicholas felt an icy hand clutch at his stomach.

"Yes. It means that there is a murderer loose in London, and that we have absolutely no idea who he is."

AFTER NICHOLAS'S startling revelation in the moonlit garden, Lavinia knew that the mood of happiness and tranquillity they had begun to feel at Rose Cottage was gone forever. The knowledge that another person had been involved in the murders—and that he was still walking free—changed everything.

For the sake of those who were not aware of the alarming news, however, she was determined to maintain an outward mien of normalcy. It would be difficult, especially given that Nicholas and Edward were planning to return to London as soon as possible to apprise Lord Osborne of the situation.

"Must you go, Nicholas?" Lavinia asked in a forlorn voice. "I am so afraid for you."

"Lord Osborne has to be made aware of this development, Lavinia," Nicholas replied gently.

"But what can you tell him? Yes, I understand that another man was there the night of the shooting, and that he is now walking freely about London, but how is that going to help you? You have no idea who he is, and until you are able to remember, of what possible use can the information be?''

Edward glanced at Nicholas and sighed. ''She's right, Nicholas. We're not much further ahead than we were before.''

''Maybe not, but does it not make sense to warn the people who were on that list so that they can at least take suitable precautions,'' Nicholas pointed out.

''Yes, I go along with that,'' Edward said. ''But there's no need for both of us to leave, my friend. I can just as easily go to London and give Osborne the news. Then it will be up to him to advise the appropriate people.'' Edward shot Nicholas a meaningful glance. ''Seems a pity to leave three such lovely young ladies here in the country—all on their own.''

Icy fingers of fear wrapped around Nicholas's heart as he realized what Edward was saying. Lavinia was one of the seven people on Leclerc's list!

A cold, black anger swept through him as he realized the danger she was in, and how relatively little he was able to do about it. Keeping his voice as emotionless as possible, he said, ''Yes, perhaps you have a point, Edward. Both of us need not go to London, and under the circumstances, it would be a pity to spoil Lavinia's plans. I think it more expedient, however, that I be the one to go to London to speak with Lord Osborne.''

"Nicholas, do you think that wise?'' Lavinia objected. "You still don't know who you're dealing with.''

"No, but then neither does Edward,'' Nicholas pointed out. "And if this signals the return of at least part of my memory, perhaps my being in London will help it along. That way, if I have another flash of insight while I'm there, I will be able to communicate with Osborne immediately. Edward, you wouldn't mind staying here with the ladies, would you? Seems a pity to cut short everyone's holiday needlessly.''

Edward nodded, fully understanding the implications in what Nicholas was saying. If there was a chance that Nicholas's memory was finally returning, he would be far better off in London than here. And under no circumstances could Lavinia be left alone now. "I wouldn't mind at all. I say, Lavinia, didn't you mention something about going to see the cathedral in Canterbury today?''

"Well, yes, but under the circumstances—''

"Good, then I shall accompany you,'' Edward said before she had a chance to finish. "Haven't been to Canterbury in an age. Charming place, as I recall.''

"I've always thought so,'' Nicholas agreed.

"But, Nicholas—"

"Yes, splendid idea," Edward carried on. "That way, the ladies will not have to postpone their outing, and you can post up to London, have your meeting and perhaps return in time for the weekend."

"But—"

"I wouldn't have to miss Lavinia's soirée."

"Gentlemen—"

"Yes, I think that would be an excellent plan."

"Gentlemen!"

Two pair of eyes swivelled towards her. "Yes, Lavinia?" Nicholas said.

"If you don't mind, Nicholas, I should like to have a small say in this matter."

He smiled at her indulgently. "But of course, my dear. We never said that you should not."

Lavinia looked at him in astonishment. "But you never allowed me to say *anything!*"

"Edward and I were just settling the arrangements in our own minds first," Nicholas told her calmly. "Do you not think my going to London and Edward escorting you to Canterbury to be a good idea?"

"I think it an excellent idea," Lavinia snapped. "I just wish someone had troubled to ask me about it first!"

IT HAD BEEN YEARS since Lavinia had been to the ancient cathedral city of Canterbury, and she was looking forward to the outing. Or at least she had been, until the plans had altered so dramatically. Her pleasure was definitely curtailed at not having Nicholas with her to share it. He had already set out for London, leaving before Martine or Laura were up. Lavinia understood his concern, of course. It was imperative that Osborne be made aware of the situation as soon as possible, hopefully before Leclerc had opportunity to strike. But that had not made her parting from Nicholas any the less painful.

Still, at least Lavinia could console herself with the knowledge that he had promised to return as soon as possible. And knowing that he was going for a good reason helped to ease the sorrow.

After Nicholas left, Lavinia and Edward returned to the breakfast parlour. Lavinia poured herself a fresh cup of coffee and then sighed. ''Oh, Edward, I can't help but feel that Nicholas is putting himself in terrible danger by going up to London.''

Edward nodded. ''Unfortunately, other people's lives are in more danger by his not going.''

Lavinia glanced at him narrowly. ''That was how you tried to justify his mission to France, and look how badly that turned out.''

"I know, but you saw for yourself how difficult it was to stop him. Nicholas takes his responsibilities very seriously. He knew the dangers inherent in his going to find Leclerc, but he also knew he was the best man available for the job. And whether we like it or not, right now Nicholas may be the only one with the ability to solve this case."

"But he *doesn't* have the ability, Edward," Lavinia cried, rising to her feet in frustration. "Not yet. Not fully. He's had only two brief glimpses into the past, neither of which have been complete. And look how long it was between the first and the second recollections. What if he goes weeks again without remembering anything, all the while being stalked by a man who wants to kill him? What protection has he against such a murderer?"

"No more than anyone, I'm afraid," Edward replied softly. "But you have to understand the gravity of the situation from Nicholas's point of view, Lavinia. If his memory is beginning to return, he is the *only* man who can find the real Leclerc. And he knows that. So do you. You know better than anyone the depths of Nicholas's loyalty."

"Yes, I do," Lavinia admitted wearily, sinking back into her chair. "And believe me, that is the only reason that allows me to accept what he is doing now."

"What are you going to tell Martine?"

Lavinia sighed. "The same thing I'm going to tell Laura. That Nicholas had some business to attend to, but that he will be back in time for the weekend."

"The soirée is this weekend, isn't it?"

Lavinia nodded. "I sent an invitation to your sister and her husband, but I haven't heard anything. They should be back any time now, I would think."

Edward chuckled. "Actually, I expected them last week. They must be having a grand time."

"They deserve it, after everything they went through," Lavinia said, recalling the misunderstandings and problems that had plagued Edward's sister and her fiancé before their wedding.

"Quite true," Edward acknowledged. "But given this most recent development, I'm not at all unhappy that they are still out of London. I hope they stay away another month. Marwood is also on Leclerc's list."

Lavinia's cheeks blanched. "Do you intend to try to get in touch with him?"

Edward poured himself another cup of coffee. "I already have."

Lavinia glanced out through the window, marvelling at how tranquil the countryside could be, untouched by the turmoil around them. "I wish to God Nicholas had never gone to France in the first place!'' she said emphatically. "Everything would be so different now."

"I don't know that it would have been, Lavinia," Edward said heavily. "Clearly, the man who shot Nicholas is as good as they come. And I have a sneaking suspicion that, had Nicholas not gone, the blackguard would be in London regardless. Our only hope is that Nicholas's memory will return fully. He's the only one who can identify the killer now."

The sound of footsteps approaching the door effectively put an end to the conversation. "Well, good morning, Lavinia, Edward," Laura said brightly. "Dear me, everyone's up already, I see. I confess, I slept like a baby again. This truly is the most peaceful place." She glanced around the room. "But where is Lord Longworth?"

"Nicholas had to return to London for a day or two, my dear," Edward informed her in a deliberately offhand manner. "Something to do with the estate. Tiresome business, but that is one of the joys of being a landowner."

"Oh dear, what a pity." Laura's face fell. "And we were to have gone to Canterbury today."

"And so we shall," Lavinia said briskly. "Except that Edward will have to act as our sole escort."

"Well, I can't think that it will trouble him unduly,'' Laura replied lightly. ''Just think, Edward, the welfare of three lovely ladies is in your hands today.''

Edward purposely did not meet Lavinia's eyes. Thank God neither of the ladies knew how true those innocent-sounding words really were.

CHAPTER NINE

NICHOLAS MADE EXCELLENT time to London. The traffic was light, and his curricle, drawn by a fleet pair of blacks, covered the distance between Rose Cottage and Town in no time at all.

Nicholas's thoughts as he raced towards London were mixed. He was pleased at having been given yet another tantalizing glimpse into his past, and the fact that it had happened so soon after he'd remembered the necklace was promising.

On the other hand, the realization that the man who had shot him and left him for dead was still on the loose terrified him. Everyone believed the danger had ended with the deaths of the other two men that night in France. Clearly, those men had been but pawns in a brutal killer's game.

Arriving in London, Nicholas went immediately to Whitehall, where he was shown into Osborne's office.

"Lord Osborne, I hope you will forgive my rather unexpected arrival."

Osborne waved his apology aside. "Think nothing of it, Longworth. Am I to assume from your hasty arrival that something of moment has taken place? Has your memory returned?''

''Not in full,'' Nicholas admitted. ''But there have been two occasions where things have come back to me. One of which is the reason I am here. I remembered something about the shooting.''

He saw Osborne tense. ''Go on.''

''There was another man there, my lord. I cannot recall anything about him, other than that he was mounted and that he shot at me from the darkness.''

There was a brief, ominous silence as the import of Nicholas's words sank in. ''Did he shoot Leclerc?'' Osborne asked finally.

''No, I shot Leclerc, or rather the man we suspected of being Leclerc. The stranger shot Ferris. And me.''

''My God!'' Osborne sank down heavily in his chair. ''Then it's true.''

Nicholas was alarmed at the note of fear in the war minister's voice. ''What's true?''

''That the man you shot was not the man we were looking for. Two nights ago, Lord Winchester was set upon and killed on the way home from his club. There were no witnesses, no clues, no suspects. He was shot at close range.'' Osborne glanced at Nicholas, his eyes dulled with worry. "You know what this means."

Nicholas nodded, his own worst suspicions confirmed. "That the man we seek *is* in London and that he's begun to carry out his threat as stated in the letter."

Osborne nodded. "Precisely. And as such, we have no time to waste. I take it you've told Kingsley."

"Yes, but not Lavinia. I thought it better not to frighten her. Edward is with her, though, and is taking every precaution."

"Good. What about Marwood?"

"As far as I know, he and Charlotte are still abroad. Edward has tried to reach him, but feels sure they will contact him as soon as they arrive back in London. He will arrange to meet them once they land."

"Fine. Then I'll contact Lord Sullivan," Osborne said. "He's the only other person on the list who isn't aware of what's happened. I'll warn him to take extra precautions for his safety until we apprehend this bastard." Osborne glanced at Nicholas again. "And you say you have absolutely no idea who the man was."

"God help me, I wish I did," he said fervently. "I can only hope it will come to me as unexpectedly as the other flashes did."

"Yes, I hope so too, Nicholas," Osborne muttered. "And without too much delay. There is a killer walking amongst us, my friend, and right now, you are the only one who knows who he is."

"That poses another problem, my lord," Nicholas said slowly.

"What's that?"

"There is a very good chance that this man knows I am alive. The fact that I have lost my memory may buy me some time, but not much. While I live, his continued safety depends on my not being able to remember what happened. Therefore, I can only conclude that whoever he is, he is likely to keep close tabs on me—to ensure that my memory doesn't return before he has taken care of me and everyone else named in the letter."

"What are you saying?"

"I am saying that if my memory does return, for the safety of all concerned, *no one* must know it but you and me."

IT WAS A STYLISH PARTY that set off from Rose Cottage a little later that morning. Lavinia had ordered the landau brought round, and with the top folded back, the passengers were given an unobstructed view of the countryside on the drive to the old cathedral town.

Lavinia was wearing a new gown of sky-blue

muslin with a matching three-quarter-length pelisse, while Martine looked delightful in a jonquil-yellow carriage gown and a demure bonnet. Laura, in deference to her favourite colour, sported an elegant ensemble in peach sarcenet with a dainty parasol of peach-and-white stripe. Edward, as the only gentleman, declined to join them in the carriage, and chose instead to accept Lavinia's offer of a spirited mount to ride alongside.

It was a lovely day, and the ride to Canterbury was a leisurely one. They reached St. Dunstan's Street on the outskirts of the city by noon, and after enjoying lunch at a very pleasant inn, they carried on through Westgate, along St. Peter's Street past the church and eventually down to the spacious cathedral grounds. Lavinia ordered the coachman to bring the carriage to a halt.

"I think a little stroll would be a good idea, don't you?"

At the chorus of agreement, she and the other ladies descended. Edward handed his horse's reins to the groom, and the party began their leisurely stroll through the grounds, Lavinia and Martine in the lead, Laura and Edward following a few paces behind.

"Oh, *c'est magnifique!* How beautiful it is!" Martine exclaimed at her first sight of the cathedral through Christ Church Gate. "And you say it is very old?"

"Yes, indeed. In fact, parts of the city date back to Roman times. Sections of the King's School and areas around it were originally monastic."

"But it is so very large. Will we be able to see it all today?"

Lavinia laughed, enjoying her stepdaughter's enthusiasm. "I hardly think so, Martine. Not and do it any justice. But we can always come back another day."

"Yes, I should like that."

The foursome continued to wander, pointing out areas of interest and generally enjoying the feeling of timelessness associated with places of great antiquity. Eventually, Laura and Edward wandered off on their own, leaving Lavinia and Martine to make their way towards The Oaks, a pretty area to the right of the cathedral.

Sitting down in the shade of a huge oak tree, Lavinia found her thoughts returning to Nicholas. She couldn't help but wonder how he was feeling. Poor man, she mused sadly. What a weight of guilt he must be carrying. He was blaming himself for having failed in his mission.

And yet he hadn't failed. He had taken care of the man they'd suspected of being Leclerc, just as he had set out to do. How was he to know that the true danger was from another person altogether?

"Well, good afternoon, Lady Duplesse, Miss Duplesse. What a pleasant coincidence this is."

Lavinia went very still, aware that what little pleasure she felt for the day had abruptly vanished. Lord Rushton was strolling across the lawn towards them.

Unfortunately, Martine was clearly not in the least displeased. "Lord Rushton!" she said brightly. *"Qu'est ce que vous—"*

"Martine!" Lavinia chided her.

"But *maman,* Lord Rushton speaks French so fluently—"

"I am well aware of that, Martine, but you are in England now, and I would thank you to remember to speak English."

Lavinia knew that her voice was sharp, but she couldn't help it. Lord Rushton seemed to bring out the worst in her. She lifted her eyes to the man in front of her. "Good afternoon, Lord Rushton. What are you doing here?"

If Rushton noticed that her voice was decidedly cool, he gave no indication of it. "I am simply enjoying the pleasure of the day, like yourselves."

"Indeed." Lavinia's smile was reserved. "I am surprised to find you so far from London."

"It is not really all that far," Rushton observed. "Besides, London is so quiet these days."

"Have you come to see the cathedral?" Martine asked, mindful of her stepmother's censure.

Rushton smiled at her with a trace of condescension. "I have seen the cathedral many times, Miss Duplesse. It holds little wonder for me now. Though seeing it through your eyes could add a new element of enjoyment. May I join you?"

Lavinia stiffened. She desperately wanted to say no, but to do so would appear the height of bad manners. After all, what could she object to? The man merely wanted to walk with them.

"If that is your wish, Lord Rushton," Lavinia said finally. "Though I fear you may find our company and our conversation sadly lacking."

"On the contrary, Lady Duplesse, how could I find the company of two such beautiful and charming ladies the least bit tiresome?"

Lavinia inclined her head at the compliment, but her feeling of disquiet remained. Especially when they began strolling again and Rushton seemed inclined to monopolize Martine's attention. He had a tendency to draw the girl away, whispering things to her and causing her to blush. When he bent his head a little too close to hers, however, Lavinia decided enough was enough.

"Come, Martine, I think we should be heading

back to the carriage. Mr. Kingsley and Miss Beaufort will be looking for us.''

Martine returned at once, but Lavinia could see that the girl was disappointed—and a little annoyed.

''Is Lord Longworth not with you today, Lady Duplesse?'' Rushton said conversationally.

''No, I fear he had to return to London unexpectedly.''

''Oh? Nothing serious, I hope. Or has he perhaps regained his memory?''

Lavinia was not sure if she detected a sudden watchfulness in his gaze. ''Unfortunately, nothing has changed in that regard, my lord. He simply needed to attend to some matters concerning the estate. He promised to return as soon as he could.'' Lavinia lowered her voice so that Martine, walking slightly ahead of them, could not hear. ''And I would remind you, Lord Rushton, that I do not approve of your attentions towards my stepdaughter. I would be grateful if you would not attempt to approach her again.''

Rushton swept her a mocking bow, but made no reply. He took a last glance at Martine, who had turned to look back at them in surprise, before pivoting on his heel and walking towards the cathedral.

"*Maman,* why are you so upset?" Martine asked when Lavinia reached her side.

"I am not upset," she replied, striving for composure. "But let us hurry. Laura and Mr. Kingsley will surely be waiting for us by now."

Lavinia said very little on the ride back to Rose Cottage. Fortunately, Martine more than made up for her stepmother's silence, filling the two-hour drive with chatter about the cathedral, the town, the old Roman buildings and their unexpected meeting with Lord Rushton. Laura cast a quick glance at Lavinia when the man's name was first mentioned, but did not ask about the incident until they were back at the house.

"Lavinia, what was Lord Rushton doing in Canterbury?"

"I don't know. He tried to say it was nothing more than a coincidence, but I have trouble believing that. And I certainly don't like the way he looks at Martine." Lavinia drew a deep breath, forcing herself to calm down. "Hopefully, after today, though, we won't be troubled by him again."

Laura moved a step closer to her. "Did you say something to Lord Rushton?"

"Yes, I did, and I would rather that you not tell Nicholas. He has enough on his plate right now. Besides, I'm probably just being…over-sensitive."

"If you are concerned about the man's intentions—"

"Laura, I want you to promise."

Her friend hesitated, clearly loath to commit to such a promise when she didn't know the extent of Lord Rushton's transgression.

"Oh, very well," she relented finally. "But if he troubles you again, I think it only right that you tell Nicholas."

"If he troubles me again, I shall," Lavinia said. "But hopefully he received my message quite clearly this afternoon!"

NICHOLAS DECIDED NOT to return to the country immediately, feeling it might be worth his while to spend a little time in London in an attempt to discover anything he could pertaining to Lord Winchester's murder. The clubs, of course, were buzzing with the news. It was generally accepted that Winchester had been set upon by a gang of footpads and killed during a robbery attempt. The fact that his purse, watch and fob were missing corroborated the story. Only a handful of people had been put wise to the true nature of Winchester's death.

It was for this reason that Nicholas retired to his club two nights later. He had hoped that through casual conversation, or even selective eavesdropping, he might learn something that would benefit him in his search. This…mystery man had to show himself sometime, and Nicholas knew it would take only a small slip for the blackguard to expose himself. Unfortunately, time was on the other man's side—time and anonymity.

"Lord Longworth, I thought I saw you come in." Lord Havermere approached Nicholas's table in a leisurely fashion. "Still no luck with the memory?"

Nicholas shook his head and put down the paper he had been perusing. "Not a bit. I begin to think the doctors were wrong. I don't think my memory is going to come back at all." He indicated the vacant chair opposite him. "Would you care to join me?"

"If you will allow me to buy you a drink?"

Nicholas inclined his head. "I wouldn't say no to a cognac, thank you."

Havermere signalled for the waiter. As he did, Nicholas studied the other man's face. "You seem in good spirits tonight, Havermere. Have you been lucky at cards or at love?"

"Neither. But then, I don't trouble myself with one and don't bother about the other. Although," Havermere said with a wink, "I might be persuaded to take Mademoiselle Chaufrière were she available."

Nicholas looked at him blankly. "Mademoiselle Chaufrière? Is she an actress?"

Havermere laughed. "My good man, she is the most exquisite Cyprian in London. Are you telling me you don't remember her, either?"

Nicholas smiled sheepishly. "I'm afraid I wouldn't know her if I fell over her."

"Dear me, you really have lost your memory. Well, it's probably just as well. A costly expense, a mistress." Havermere smiled urbanely. "Especially for a man contemplating marriage. Speaking of which, this memory loss must be a dashed nuisance with regards to your lovely fiancée."

"How do you mean?"

"Well, one minute ready to marry the woman, the next not even remembering who she is. Bit of a turnabout, I should think."

Nicholas's smile could have meant anything. "I just have to start over again, as they say. Fortunately, Lavinia is being most patient with me."

Havermere's smile was smug. "You mean in giving you time to fall in love with her again?"

Resentment sharpened Nicholas's voice. "That's not what I meant."

"Now, now, Longworth, there's no need to fly up in the boughs," Havermere said quickly. "All I'm saying is that when a man loses his memory, the good memories as well as the bad are lost, are they not?"

"The feelings that inspired the good memories can be recreated," Nicholas said. "Which is why Lavinia and I decided not to break off our betrothal. We are giving ourselves time for those feelings to develop."

"And if they do not?"

Nicholas's face was carefully expressionless. "I have every reason to believe that they will."

Havermere shrugged eloquently. "Love takes a long time to grow."

"I have time enough, Havermere."

"Yes, I suppose." Havermere poured out two glasses of cognac. "You are a fortunate man, Longworth."

Nicholas smiled, but his eyes were cool. "All things considered, yes, I suppose I am."

"The stepdaughter, Martine, is charming. And so devoted to her stepmother. She reminds me of her father, though. Did you know François Duplesse?"

"If I did, I don't remember."

"But of course, I keep forgetting," Havermere said with a laugh. "Forgive me. It's just so hard to imagine not being able to remember anything. People, places, even voices."

"As I said, a complete blank."

They made desultory conversation for a few more minutes. Then, as the clock in the hall struck twelve, Havermere looked up in surprise. "Dear me, is it that time already? I must take myself off. Told Rushton I'd meet him at The Club House before midnight."

Nicholas glanced at the man. "The Club House?"

"Yes. On Bennet Street." Havermere winked. "One of the less-respectable places for a gentleman to be seen, but there's always something of interest going on. You never know who you're going to bump into." He smiled down at Nicholas as he stood up. "Lovely chatting with you, old boy. Do keep me informed as to the memory. Oh, please stay and have another cognac, on me."

Nicholas picked up his newspaper as soon as Havermere left. But when the door closed behind him, he slowly lowered it again. The man had been pumping him. No, more than that, he had been testing him, trying to trip him up on his knowledge of the Cyprian, and of François Duplesse.

But why? Why would Lord Havermere be interested in trying to find out how much he was able to remember? And why the sudden interest in Lavinia? Nicholas hadn't failed to note the admiration in Havermere's voice when he'd spoken of her. Admiration and…desire?

Jealousy slammed into Nicholas's stomach like a blow from an iron fist. Bloody hell! Was it possible that Havermere was interested in Lavinia? Was he hoping that Lavinia might tire of him, and eventually start looking for someone else? Was that why he had been testing him? Baiting him?

Nicholas felt his mood veer sharply towards anger. The more he thought about it, the more sense it made. It would certainly explain the watchfulness in Havermere's eyes—and his questions regarding Nicholas's memory. No doubt Havermere hoped his memory might never return, and that eventually Lavinia would get tired of waiting. Maybe Havermere saw himself as the one she might eventually turn to!

He picked up the bottle of cognac Havermere had so graciously provided and poured himself another glass. ''In a pig's bloody eye!'' he swore softly.

TRUE TO HIS WORD, Nicholas did return before the weekend. He found Lavinia and her guests in the drawing-room, playing cards. Martine was reading a book on the settee and was the first to spot him. ''Nicholas, you're back!''

Lavinia glanced up from her cards. Resisting the urge to rush headlong into his arms, she gracefully rose and held out her hand to him. "Nicholas, was everything all right in London?"

"Everything was...much as I expected." His smile slipped for no more than a moment, long enough for Edward to realize that something was wrong.

"Well, we have missed you."

"Oh, yes, Nicholas, we had such a lovely time in Canterbury," Martine said. "I must tell you all about it."

"And you will, my dear, but perhaps not right now," Lavinia said gently. She had noticed the worry in her fiancé's eyes the moment he had stepped into the room. "I think perhaps Nicholas is tired after his journey."

He smiled at her gratefully. "Yes, I confess I am weary. It seems I am not as recovered from my injuries as I would like to think."

Martine was all contrition. "Oh, *pardon,* Nicholas, *je ne pensais pas—*"

"Martine," Lavinia reminded her.

"Oh, bother!" the girl groaned, using a very English expression indeed. "I was just so eager to tell you about it."

"And tell me you shall, Martine, for I am anxious to hear," Nicholas said kindly. "I know, we shall discuss it over breakfast, you and I. Would you like that?"

"Oh, yes, I would like that very much."

"Good." Nicholas turned to greet Lavinia. "And how is my favourite hostess?"

Lavinia laughed, and blushed prettily. "Very well, now that all her guests are returned."

"Yes, and in good time for the soirée, too," Laura observed.

"I told you I would be back in time," Nicholas said. "Edward, I wonder if I might have a word with you. I bumped into an old friend of yours while I was in Town. He wanted me to pass along a message for you."

"Did he indeed? Well, I am consumed with curiosity." Edward rose and bowed to the ladies. "If you will excuse me."

"Ladies," Nicholas said.

When they had gone, Laura turned to Lavinia with a long-suffering smile. "I vow, it is just the same with those two as it was with Edward and Lord Marwood. Always disappearing together somewhere, always talking about things."

"What things?"

"Oh, I don't know. Things we're not supposed to know about. Matters concerning Lord Osborne, most of the time," Laura admitted. "Charlotte did warn me that I would have to get used to it if I hoped to marry Edward. Of course, at the time, I never thought I would be fortunate enough to…

That is, I had no idea he felt...that way,'' she finished, blushing.

Lavinia smiled. ''Well, he obviously did. But I do know what you mean about the two of them disappearing. Just once, I would like to be a fly on the wall when Edward and Nicholas are discussing business.''

''WINCHESTER KILLED?'' Edward repeated in a shocked. voice. ''But how did it happen? And when?''

''A few nights ago. Made to look like a robbery. One bullet fired at close range.'' Nicholas sighed. ''Winchester never had a chance, poor blighter.''

''Why are they calling it robbery?''

''His purse was taken, as well as his gold watch and fob. The killer obviously wanted everyone to think it was a simple robbery.''

Edward drew a heavy breath. ''Then it's begun.''

''So it would seem. Osborne has warned Sullivan, and with Winchester dead, that just leaves Osborne, Marwood and the three of us.''

''I hope to God Charlotte and Devon decide to prolong their wedding trip,'' Edward muttered. ''Not a pleasant thought, coming back to find that someone is trying to kill you.''

''We'll just have to get word to Marwood as

soon as he does return. As for the rest of us, I think we had better keep in very close contact.''

''Nicholas, do you think it's wise not to tell Lavinia of the danger she's in? I mean, I understand that you don't want her to worry, but surely she has a right to protect herself. You can't do that for her.''

''I can to the best of my ability.''

''Yes, but you're not with her all the time,'' Edward pointed out. ''It would be a lot easier if you were married, of course, but given that you're not...''

''Yes, I know.'' Nicholas thought about it for a few minutes. ''And you're right. I suppose it is only fitting that she know. I've asked Osborne to have one of his men keep an eye on her house in London. I want to know everyone who goes in and out of there.''

''I think that's a good idea.'' Edward took a sip of brandy from the glass he had brought in with him. ''Anything else of interest happen while you were gone?''

''Yes, now that you ask,'' Nicholas said, unable to prevent the chill from entering his voice. ''I went to the club the other night, hoping to stumble across something, when Havermere came up and started chatting to me. He left around midnight for a place called The Club House.''

"The Club House!" Edward frowned. "I say, that's a bit seedy for the likes of Havermere. Didn't think he'd be the type to frequent the hells."

"Well, I don't know about that. He said he was meeting Rushton."

"Rushton?" Edward sat up. "Now that is a coincidence. Lavinia told me that she and Martine bumped into him in Canterbury the other day."

Nicholas glanced at him quickly. "What would Rushton be doing in Canterbury?"

"I don't know. Why don't you ask Lavinia?"

Nicholas's hand closed tightly around the stem of his glass. "Yes, I think perhaps I shall."

CHAPTER TEN

NICHOLAS DECIDED NOT TO broach the subject of
Lord Rushton with Lavinia that night. He was surprisingly tired after the trip from London and
turned in early. But once again his sleep was restless, punctuated by dreams of faceless people, all
of whom spoke in low, monotone voices. He
tossed endlessly, trying to find escape from the im-
ages, but they were always there, waiting for him
when he drifted off again.

Consequently, when he awoke the next morning,
he had dark shadows under his eyes and was in a
less-than-amiable frame of mind. Recalling that he
had promised to talk with Martine, however, he
reluctantly rose, and with his valet's help, eventually made his way downstairs, hoping to enjoy a
fortifying cup of coffee before she arrived.

Martine was already there. "Good morning,
Nicholas," she greeted him brightly. "I have been
waiting for you."

Nicholas regarded her in wry amusement. "My

dear girl, it is far too early to be about. You should still be abed.''

"You are not."

"Of course not, but gentlemen generally do not linger in their beds as long as ladies."

"Well, I do not linger in bed, either," Martine asserted. "I knew we were to talk this morning. Would you like me to pour you some coffee?"

Nicholas smiled ruefully. "Yes, thank you, that would be lovely."

He watched as she handled the silver pot with a grace not unlike Lavinia's. "There you are," she said, handing him the cup.

"Thank you, Martine. Now, tell me about your trip to Canterbury."

"Oh, it was so lovely, Nicholas. The cathedral, the Roman wall. It has such a sense of history, *n'est-ce pas?*"

"Does that surprise you?"

Martine tilted her head to one side. "No. I know that England is a very old country. It is like France in that way. Have you seen Versailles, Nicholas?"

"I'm afraid I don't know, Martine. I assume it is very impressive."

"*Oui,* it is. And I felt that same kind of emotion when I saw the cathedral, which is so very beautiful. There were many young ladies sketching."

"What else happened on your trip, Martine?"

Nicholas asked casually. "I understand you met someone."

He noted the colour deepening in the girl's cheeks. "Yes, we saw...Lord Rushton."

Nicholas took a sip of coffee. "And how did that come about?"

"*Maman* and I were sitting on a bench and he walked right up to us. Isn't that a coincidence— that he would be there on the very same day?"

"A coincidence indeed." Nicholas set his cup on the table. "Did Lord Rushton say why he was in Canterbury?"

"He mentioned that he liked to get away from Town now and then. He said London was very quiet just now."

Quiet? A prominent peer killed in a supposed robbery and Rushton called that quiet? Interesting.

"Tell me, Martine, did Lord Rushton talk to Lavinia at all?"

Martine's smile faded. "Yes, but I do not think *maman* likes Lord Rushton, Nicholas. I heard them talking just before he left and I think she was angry."

"Did you hear what they were talking about?"

"No. I was walking a little ahead of them. But when I turned around, I saw Lord Rushton bow and then walk away."

Nicholas phrased his next question carefully. "Martine, apart from the time you met Lord Rushton in London, and the other day at Canterbury, have you seen the gentleman any other time?''

Nicholas knew he had his answer when the girl's face flushed crimson. ''I see you have. When, Martine?''

''I did not do anything wrong, Nicholas.''

''I'm not saying you did, my dear, but I would like to know how it is you and Lavinia keep running into Lord Rushton. Where did you see him the other time?''

Martine bit her lip. ''He was…in the village. I told *maman* I wanted to get some ribbon for my bonnet.''

''I see. So you met him there. Did he arrange that?''

Martine nodded guiltily. ''Yes. Before we left London.''

Nicholas tried not to show his anger. He didn't like what he was hearing. ''Martine, does Lord Rushton…ask you anything about Lavinia, or myself?''

''Oh yes, Nicholas, he is most concerned about you. He always asks how you are feeling, and if your memory has returned.''

Nicholas felt the hair on the back of his neck rise. ''You didn't tell him about the necklace, did you?''

Martine blushed. ''I nearly did, but then I remembered that you said not to tell anyone in case it got their hopes up.''

''That's right, Martine. I wouldn't want to raise anyone's hopes needlessly.'' *Or suspicions.* ''For that reason, it is very important that we keep the information to ourselves, all right?''

''Yes, Nicholas, I promise.''

''That's my girl.''

''Nicholas?''

''Yes?''

''Have you remembered…anything else?''

Nicholas shook his head, convinced that it was better for everyone that she not know. ''I'm afraid not, Martine. But I am still hopeful.''

The door to the breakfast parlour opened and they both turned as Lavinia entered. ''So this is where the two of you are,'' she said. ''I looked in your room, Martine, but Hélène said you had already gone down. I might have known you were meeting a gentleman.''

''I just wanted to tell Nicholas about our trip. And now that I have, may I be excused?''

''Where are you off to now?''

''The big white cat in the stable has had kittens, and Jim said he would show them to me.''

''Jim?'' Nicholas enquired.

Lavinia chuckled. ''My old groom. All right, Martine, off you go.''

Martine dashed out of the room, leaving Nicholas and Lavinia behind to smile at each other. "One minute an elegant young lady, the next, a giggling girl off to see kittens." Lavinia shook her head. "I never quite know where I am with her."

"I suppose that's one of the joys of motherhood."

"Mmm, I'm afraid I didn't have much of a run up to it, though," Lavinia admitted. "By the time I came on the scene, most of Martine's growing up had already been done."

Nicholas laced his fingers together on the table. "She still needs you, Lavinia. She's not as sure of herself as she likes to make out."

"Yes, I know. But then, at other times, she seems so dreadfully mature that I really feel quite helpless beside her. Lately, I have begun to feel that there is a distance growing between us. She isn't telling me…everything that's going on in her life." Lavinia fingered the lace edge of the tablecloth and glanced at Nicholas. "Nicholas, what do you think of…Lord Rushton?"

"Rushton?" Nicholas schooled his expression to one of neutrality. "Why do you ask?"

"Because I think that Martine is…intrigued by him," she said carefully.

"Do you mean infatuated?"

Lavinia blushed. She should have known better. Nicholas—even without his memory—was a very astute man. "Yes, I suppose. I know they haven't had much to do with each other, but—"

"On the contrary, Lavinia, they've had more contact than you think." Nicholas proceeded to tell Lavinia what Martine had confided.

"Nicholas, I don't like this," Lavinia said, unable to hide her concern any longer. "It bothers me that the man always seems to be laying in wait for her."

"Is that what you think he's doing?" Nicholas enquired.

"Yes. And I'm afraid I've not been very subtle about my own reservations towards him."

He drew a long breath. "Lavinia, what do you know about Rushton?"

"Next to nothing," she admitted. "He claims to have known François and his family, but it must have been long before I married him. I never heard François mention the man."

"And did Martine remember ever having seen him about the house?"

"No, but she was probably quite young when Lord Rushton was visiting."

"But why does he seem so interested in her all of a sudden? And why does he keep on asking her about my memory?"

Lavinia sighed. "I can only think that his interest in Martine stems from the fact that she is an extremely pretty girl and of marriageable age, though it pains me to think so in this case. As for his interest in you, I assume it arises from the same thing. He knows how close the two of you are. Perhaps he hopes to work his way into her heart by affecting an interest in you.''

Unfortunately, Nicholas knew that affecting an interest was all it really was. He no more thought Lord Rushton was genuinely concerned about his welfare than he believed that the man's bumping into Lavinia and Martine in Canterbury the other day had been a coincidence. Too many incidents involving the mysterious Lord Rushton were being labelled "coincidental" for his liking.

NICHOLAS'S FEELINGS OF uncertainty grew. He recognized that his insecurities were getting far too strong a hold on him. There had been no more elusive flashes of memory. Even his dreams were growing more nebulous. For the first time since his return to London, Nicholas truly began to fear that his memory lapse would turn out to be permanent.

"Lavinia, I think I should…go back to London for a while.''

The suggestion came like a bolt out of the blue, catching Lavinia totally unawares. They had gone out for an early afternoon ride to enjoy the weather and had dismounted to walk in companionable silence, though Lavinia was well aware that Nicholas's mind was far from restful. She could read the play of emotions on his face like an open book.

"Go back to London?" she repeated. "But why? Are you tired of Rose Cottage?"

He shook his head. "I don't think anyone could ever tire of this place," he admitted softly. "No, it has nothing to do with Rose Cottage. Or with you," he said, before she had a chance to suggest it.

"Then why do you wish to leave?"

Nicholas stopped walking, forcing Lavinia to do the same. "I don't know exactly. I just sense that something should be happening. I feel that by staying out here in the countryside, I'm missing something, that I'm not going to be able to make it happen."

"Make what happen, Nicholas?" Lavinia asked. Then her face went pale. "Have you had another flashback?"

"No. There's been nothing. But I can't help but feel that it's just there beyond my reach, waiting for me to grab it." He turned and looked at her earnestly. "I know why you wanted me to come here, Lavinia, and believe me, I thought it was a good idea, too. But it hasn't worked—not the way we wanted it to. Now I think it's time to try another tactic."

Lavinia stared at him in puzzlement. "What other tactic?"

"One I probably should have used earlier," Nicholas admitted. "But I can't do it here. I have to go back to London."

"Then I will come back with you," she said immediately.

"Oh, no, you won't." Nicholas was adamant. "You're far safer in the country."

"Safer?" Lavinia glanced at him and chuckled. "Why wouldn't I be safe in Town?"

Nicholas bit his lip. That had been an unfortunate slip. He still wasn't sure he wanted Lavinia to know she was on Leclerc's list. "Look, Lavinia, I understand what you're trying to do, but this is something I think I'm going to have to do for myself. You've done everything humanly possible. Now it's my turn."

Lavinia glanced at him with huge, worried eyes. "And what about…us, Nicholas? Is it time to do something about that, too?"

Nicholas turned and gazed into her eyes, seeing the hurt, the worry, the pain clouding them. He shook his head.

"No. My relationship with you hasn't been given a chance to develop. Not while I've been so busy trying to reestablish who *I* am. I want to give us all the time we deserve."

Lavinia smiled sadly. "Perhaps there is no need, Nicholas. You said you fell in love with me at first sight. If it is taking you so long to make up your mind this time, perhaps I already have my answer.''

They rode back to Rose Cottage in silence. Watching her, Nicholas couldn't help but feel that she had just taken the first, tiny step away from him. The thought caused him more pain than he could have imagined possible.

NICHOLAS MET WITH EDWARD later that same night. He knew his friend was planning on returning to London in two days. But when Nicholas told him that he would be leaving, too, there was no mistaking the surprise on Edward's face.

''But why?'' he asked, puzzled at the abrupt turn of events. ''Has something happened?''

''No, but I now realize that nothing is going to as long as I remain here.'' He ran his fingers through his dark hair in frustration. ''There's a killer walking free in London, Edward. A killer that only I can recognize. I'm never going to be able to identify him by sitting here in Kent. There's nothing else for it. I *must* return to London.''

''That's all very well, my friend, but the problem is you *can't* recognize him. You wouldn't know him if he walked up and slapped you across the face.''

Nicholas shook his head. ''Not at the moment, no. But I refuse to believe the situation won't change. If there hadn't been those two instances, I would feel more inclined to believe there's no hope. But I know differently. If something has come back to me from the past, other things will, too!''

''All right. What do you intend to do?''

''I intend to be as visible as possible,'' Nicholas told him. ''I intend to go back to London and be seen in public as much as I can. The more I hear, the more I'll learn. And the more I learn, the more likely I'll be to stumble upon something that will trigger my memory.''

''You realize that we're going to have to change some plans,'' Edward said. ''We can't both go back to London and leave the ladies here.''

''No. I originally told Lavinia that she should stay here, but I think it better that we all return to London together. Lavinia has planned this soirée for Saturday night, and I'm not going to disappoint her by leaving. But I think we had best be prepared to leave Sunday, or Monday at the latest.''

Edward nodded in agreement. ''All right, if you're sure. But it may look rather obvious if we all leave together. Perhaps Laura and I should leave Sunday, then you can follow with Lavinia and Martine early in the week.''

''Good idea. We have to move very carefully now, Edward. Until we know exactly who we're dealing with, we can't afford to take any chances.

If the murderer gets even a hint that we're on to him, the results could be devastating!''

LAVINIA SAT in her bedroom and put the finishing touches on her toilette, trying to ignore the words of doubt the voice in the back of her mind was whispering.

Something is going on. Something terrible is about to happen. Someone is going to get hurt.

Yes, something was happening, and it had to do with Nicholas. Just as she had felt a premonition the night he had been shot, so Lavinia felt tension mounting again. The only difference was that this time the sensation of danger was not focused. This time, it seemed to be all around her, and try as she might, she could not shake the feeling.

She turned at the sound of a knock on her door. ''Come in, Martine.'' The door swung open, but it was not her stepdaughter who stood on the threshold. ''Nicholas!''

Nicholas took in the sight of Lavinia sitting at her dressing-table, noting the elegantly upswept hairstyle, the richness of the emerald-green gown and the compassion and intelligence in the bright blue eyes. He couldn't help but marvel that this beautiful woman was actually bothering to wait for him.

She could have had her pick from among dozens of men, all of whom she knew, all of whom knew her. And many, Nicholas was quickly finding out, would have been very happy to take his place at her side—Havermere first and foremost. It was not an encouraging thought.

"Have you nothing to say to me this evening, my lord?" Lavinia flashed a slow, seductive smile. "Does my appearance not meet with your approval?"

Nicholas took a deep breath. "I fear that nothing I could say would seem sufficient. You quite literally defy words."

A warmth flashed in her eyes. "How is it, Nicholas, that even when you do not use traditional words of flattery, I feel that I have been complimented far more than if you had?"

He laughed, the sound a throaty, masculine chuckle. "Because hopefully, I am able to communicate more by the manner in which I say things than by the words I use."

"Yes, I would say you succeed quite admirably at that." Lavinia reached for her fan and looped its silk cord around her wrist. "Shall we go?" She saw the momentary hesitation in his eyes. "Nicholas? Is something wrong?"

"Wrong? No, of course not," he said, abruptly changing his mind. He had been about to tell her that they would all be leaving when the weekend was over, but decided against it. There would be time enough when the evening was done. "Come, my dear, your guests await."

Lavinia slipped her hand through his arm. "On the contrary, Nicholas, *our* guests await."

With Martine's help, the servants had decorated Rose Cottage so that it resembled something out of a fairy tale. Hundreds of candles illuminated the entry and main reception rooms, while lengths of rose-coloured silk draping the walls cast a warm glow over everything. It was a cosy, intimate feeling, and Nicholas knew that it was a reflection of Lavinia herself.

As for his fiancée, Nicholas found himself watching her frequently throughout the course of the evening. His eyes returned to her time and again, drawn by the sound of her laughter, held by the richness of her beauty.

When she eventually returned to his side, she was touched by the admiration she saw on his face. "Are you having a good time?"

"I am, because you are a consummate hostess, Lavinia Duplesse," Nicholas murmured. He tucked her hand into his arm and led her out through the French doors onto the terrace, where hundreds of tiny candles glowed like stars. "There is a tremendous feeling of warmth in this house tonight, and it is all because of you."

Lavinia tried not to show how much his words moved her. "You give me far too much credit, my dear. It is simply that you are enjoying yourself. You feel no pressure, and you know you are with friends.''

Nicholas glanced back towards the crowded room. ''Yes, you are fortunate to have gathered such a congenial group of people around you. I have not heard one unkind remark about anyone tonight.'' He chuckled ruefully. ''I did not think it was possible.''

Lavinia's laughter was as clear and light as a bell. ''Oh Nicholas, not everyone is out to impress, or to criticize. I should almost think that that is one of the few benefits of your condition—you are forming all your opinions again.''

''Lavinia, there you are,'' Anthony Hewitt said. ''I thought I heard your voice. And Lord Longworth, good evening.''

''Evening, Hewitt. A pleasure to see you again.''

The two men shook hands warmly. ''Actually, it was you I wanted to see, Lord Longworth. I understand you are recently returned from London. No doubt you heard about that nasty bit of business with Lord Winchester.''

Lavinia turned to Anthony in surprise. ''Oh? What happened?''

''You didn't hear about the robbery?''

Nicholas quickly spoke up. ''It need not concern you, Lavinia. Unfortunately, footpads and thieves are as common as streetwalkers in London after dark."

"Thieves are one thing, Longworth," Anthony agreed, "but murderers are another altogether."

Lavinia blanched. "Murderers! Dear Lord, has someone been killed?"

"Yes. Poor old Winchester. Set upon by a gang of thieves. Had his purse and watch taken, and then was shot dead. I tell you, it is no longer safe to walk the streets," Hewitt commented ruefully. "The next time I go up to London, I shall make damn sure I don't step out of my... Lavinia! Are you all right?"

Nicholas turned, and grabbed his fiancée's arm just as she swayed forward. "Lavinia!"

"I'm...all right," she said weakly, avoiding his eyes.

"Perhaps you would like to go and lie down for a while," Nicholas suggested.

She looked at him then, her gaze probing. "Yes, I think that might be a good idea. I am sure it is just the excitement of the evening."

"Hewitt, will you excuse us?"

"Yes, of course. I hope it wasn't something I said, Lavinia," he added belatedly. "I didn't mean to upset you."

Lavinia managed a weak smile. "No, you did not. And I'm fine. Really. Nicholas, why don't you stay here with Anthony. I'll just take a few moments alone. Pray do not tell anyone.''

''Of course not.'' He escorted her as far as the bottom of the stairs. ''Are you sure you can manage on your own?''

She heard the genuine note of concern in his voice, but shook her head. She was beginning to realize why she had sensed danger before. ''Quite sure.'' She turned and met his gaze. ''Though I wish you had been truthful with me earlier.''

Nicholas felt the weight of his deception more fully. ''I did not wish to alarm you.''

Lavinia nodded, and then slowly turned and made her way upstairs. So, there was more going on than Nicholas had told her about. It didn't surprise her. It explained why he had been so quiet since his return from London. It explained why he had closeted himself with Edward the moment he'd returned. And it explained the look of concern she had glimpsed in his eyes earlier.

A murderer was stalking British agents in London. He'd already killed Winchester, and had promised to kill more. And as long as Nicholas's memory was gone, the villain could waltz undetected through the drawing-rooms of Society. He could laugh and share a joke with anyone—before pulling out a pistol and cold-bloodedly shooting them dead. And only Nicholas knew who he was.

Dear God, was it any wonder the poor man was suffering so?

THE SOIRÉE WAS OVER. The last of the guests had gone. Martine had retired to her room, leaving Laura, Edward, Nicholas and Lavinia in the drawing-room. Their faces reflected the gravity of the situation.

"So this is why you want us to return to London," Lavinia said quietly. She spoke without noticeable inflection and directed her question towards Nicholas, who nodded tersely.

"I think it best," he answered. "Osborne has warned Sullivan of the danger, and they are both taking extra precautions. But as they have voiced their intention of remaining in London, it seems likely that the murderer will stay there, too."

"Then why do you need to be there?" Laura's voice shook as she turned to Edward. "Surely it would be safer for you and Nicholas if you were distanced from the others."

"On the contrary, Laura," Edward replied, "we probably stand a better chance of catching the man if we are all in the same area. We can observe other peoples' movements."

"Staying in London didn't help Lord Winchester," Laura retaliated stubbornly.

"No, but then Winchester was completely unsuspecting," Nicholas said in a saddened voice.

"What gentleman has not walked through the London streets after dark at some time or other?"

"When would you like us to be ready to leave?" Lavinia enquired.

Nicholas silently blessed his fiancée's level-headedness. "Edward and I have already discussed this. We don't want to make it look too obvious, so he and Laura will return tomorrow. I thought perhaps you, Martine and I could return Tuesday."

Lavinia nodded. "We'll be ready."

"Well, in that case, I think I had better turn in," Laura said. "Tomorrow will be a busy day. I shall have my maid start packing first thing."

Nicholas smiled. "Thank you, Laura. And I am sorry to have brought this idyllic stay to such an abrupt end."

"Well, at least we were able to enjoy it for a while," Laura said charitably. "Good night all."

"Good night." Edward slowly rose, stretching his long limbs. "I suppose I'd best turn in, too. We can make the rest of the arrangements in the morning."

Nicholas nodded. "Yes. Good night, Edward."

When they were alone, Lavinia turned her gaze on Nicholas. "You didn't tell me the truth, did you?"

He studied her carefully. "What do you mean?"

She rose and made her way to his side, sinking down on the carpet by his feet, just as she had done the first time he had seen her upon his return from France. "You didn't tell me the names of all of the people on Leclerc's list."

At his look of dismay, she smiled rather sadly. "You shouldn't be surprised, Nicholas. One of the things you used to admire most about me was my intuitiveness, and I fear that has not changed. My name is on that list, too, isn't it?"

When he didn't answer, Lavinia gave a brief, mirthless laugh. "Of course it is. It would have to be, being that I was married to François. They tried to get me after they killed my husband, but I managed to escape. Why should I think that this man would not want to settle the score with me now?"

Nicholas reached for her hands and raised them both to his lips. "I didn't want to frighten you, Lavinia. And until Winchester was killed, I wasn't even sure we had any reason to be concerned. But as soon as Osborne told me, I knew that the danger existed. And until we find this man, I can't afford to have you here where I can't protect you."

"You don't have to explain, Nicholas, I understand why we have to return. But it doesn't mean I feel any better about it. Do you realize the kind of danger you're putting yourself in?"

"Yes." Nicholas met her gaze directly. "But as long as I have no recollection of what happened, I pose no immediate threat to the killer. He's playing a game of cat and mouse. He knows I can't get away, but he's not ready to kill me just yet.''

''Dear God, don't say that!'' Lavinia shut her eyes.

''But it's true. That is why I told Osborne that, even if my memory does return, no one must know but him and me. It's the only way to ensure my safety, and ultimately yours.''

Lavinia searched his face. ''Has your memory returned, Nicholas? Surely you can tell me.''

He shook his head. ''No, it hasn't,'' he growled. ''In truth, I don't know that it ever will. There hasn't been anything since the last time. Not a flash, not a premonition, not even a—a feeling that I was getting closer to recapturing my past. Don't you see, Lavinia, that's another reason why I have to go back. I have to make something happen. I have to force the issue!''

''But you can't force it!'' she cried. ''You've already seen that. The harder you try, the more elusive your memory becomes.''

''Then I have to stop relying on my memory,'' he told her quietly. ''I was a good agent before this happened. I have to believe that part of my ability came from within, from my own instincts and reactions. I have to confront this devil and the only place I can do that is in London. I know he's there, Lavinia. And one way or another, I'll track him down. For all of our sakes, I have to!''

EDWARD AND LAURA LEFT around noon the following day. Nicholas, Martine and Lavinia waved them off, and then returned to the house to continue their own packing. Martine had been saddened to learn that they would be returning to London, but had accepted it with the perpetual optimism of youth.

"You're not too disappointed, I hope, Martine," Lavinia said as they walked back to the house.

"Not really. I love Rose Cottage, and I look forward to coming back here again, but I am anxious to get back to London, too." The girl's eyes shone brightly. "There is so much to see and do in Town. Parties to go to, shops to buy pretty things in."

"And the company of handsome young gentlemen?" Lavinia asked. She was amused to see the blush that suffused her stepdaughter's cheeks. Thankfully, there had been no more mention of Lord Rushton. But Martine was growing up quickly. "Never mind, I will not tease you. But I am glad you are not unhappy about leaving here."

"Are you sorry to leave, *maman?*" Martine asked.

Lavinia glanced at the ivy-covered walls of Rose Cottage and nodded. "Yes, I am. This is a peaceful place, and I feel its serenity like a soothing balm.

I feel that…nothing bad could ever happen here.''
She shook her head, wishing she could say the
same for London.

BY WEDNESDAY NIGHT, Rose Cottage was just a
memory. Lavinia and Martine were once again settled in the town house in London, and Nicholas
had returned to his bachelor premises. He had gone
to see Lord Osborne immediately upon his return.
Edward was already there, waiting for him. But the
news was not good.

"Sullivan's dead," Osborne told him without
preamble.

"Dead!" Nicholas gasped. "But what in blazes
happened? I thought you were going to warn him."

"I did. He was killed during a hunt. Apparently,
he fell from his horse and broke his neck."

"So he wasn't murdered."

Edward drummed his fingers on the desk. "We
don't know that for sure, Nicholas. It could have
been disguised to look like an accident. I doubt our
killer will want to make things too obvious."

"Humph. Damn difficult to make a murder look
innocent," Osborne grumbled.

"Difficult, but not impossible." Nicholas studied the fine painting of a race horse on the wall
behind Osborne's desk. Strange that he hadn't noticed it the last time he'd been here. "When you
think about it, even something as simple as a riding
fatality could be made to look like an accident."

Osborne raised an eyebrow. "You're not making me feel any better about this, Longworth."

"Sorry, my lord, but when you consider that the man is a trained killer, you realize he'd hardly resort to obvious means to dispatch his victims."

"Well, I suppose there's nothing we can do but maintain a careful watch and ensure that none of us on that list are left alone at any time," Edward said. "Not even in our homes."

"Yes, I've no doubt that this man is capable of breaking into houses," Nicholas observed grimly.

"If that's the case, I wonder if it's a good idea for Lavinia and Martine to be left alone in theirs," Osborne said suddenly. "Seems to me it would be a good deal safer to have them living somewhere else for a while."

Nicholas cursed himself for not having thought of that sooner.

"Damn it, you're right. But where? I'd move them into my place, but I hate to think what the Town would say."

"You and Lavinia could always get married," Edward suggested.

Nicholas glanced at him in astonishment. "Married?"

"Well, think about it. It's a perfect solution. You and Lavinia seem to be getting on extremely well, and you certainly like Martine."

"Yes, but—"

"And the banns have already been read. You could be married immediately. Then you could move both of them into your house, giving them the extra protection they need."

"I say, that's not a bad idea," Osborne said suddenly. "And it could work both ways. You could protect Lavinia, and Lavinia could protect you."

"Protect me?" Nicholas stared at him. "How in the world could she protect me?"

"Simply by being there, my friend," Edward explained. "Right now you live alone with just a valet, a cook and a butler in the house. If you were married, Lavinia would be there with you, too. All the time."

"It would also allow the two of you to be seen together," Osborne said. "Whenever Lavinia went out in the evening, it would be with you. And in the daytime, you could have a footman accompany her. But at least you would know that every night she would be coming back to your house."

Nicholas's mind was in turmoil. Marry Lavinia? He'd been so caught up in trying to regain his memory that he'd never really stopped to think about how far their relationship had developed. Did he love the woman enough to spend the rest of his life with her?

More important, was he willing to take the chance that she might not be alive if he *didn't* marry her?

"YOU'RE ASKING ME to...marry you?" Lavinia stared at Nicholas in shock. "But...are you sure?"

"It is something I have given a lot of thought to, Lavinia, and I think it would be a good idea." Nicholas tried not to smile at the look of surprise on her face. "Or perhaps you have had a change of heart yourself."

Lavinia swallowed and quickly shook her head. "N-no, my feelings on the matter have not... changed, Nicholas. It's just that I am somewhat...surprised to hear that you've come to this decision so abruptly, that's all. Dear me, this is most unexpected."

Nicholas smiled and walked towards the settee where she sat. "I understand that the banns have already been read."

"Yes, of course. Before you went away, in fact." Lavinia felt herself blush. "I wasn't going to say anything but...we were to have been married in just a few days time."

"How marvellous. Then we still can be."

"What?" she gasped.

"Well, I see no point in waiting. Do you?"

Lavinia could hardly believe this was happening. "Well, no, I suppose not, but—"

"And then, as soon as we are married, you and Martine can come to live with me," he informed her.

That brought Lavinia up short. "Live with you? But…where?"

"Where? Where do you think? At my house, of course."

"That's very good of you, Nicholas, but I hardly think there will be room enough for everyone. You are living in bachelor's quarters, after all."

Nicholas thought for a moment. "Well, there is the house in Mayfair. I'm sure mother would not mind."

"Perhaps, but I rather doubt she would welcome all of us on such short notice." Lavinia hesitated a moment. "Would you consider living here?"

"Here?" Nicholas glanced around him. He thought for a moment. It might not be a bad idea at that. There was a good deal more traffic on this road than on his own. More difficult for someone to break in unobserved.

"Yes, that might not be a bad idea. At least temporarily. We would, of course, look for something more suitable at the first opportunity."

Lavinia looked into his face and shook her head. "Why, Nicholas? Why all of a sudden like this? It has something to do with this man, doesn't it?" she enquired softly.

"Lavinia, it has nothing to do with—"

"You want to…protect me, don't you? And the best way for you to do that is to have me living with you. Is that right, Nicholas? Is that what prompted this sudden declaration of marriage?''

Nicholas hesitated, not sure of the answer himself. ''It is not the only reason, no. But would it be such a bad reason if it were?''

Lavinia shrugged gracefully. ''It would not be the worst reason I have heard, of course, but neither would it be the best.'' She studied his face with loving eyes. ''Do you remember how you proposed to me the first time?''

He shook his head wistfully. ''Sadly, I do not.''

''You were terribly romantic.'' Lavinia's eyes softened as her memory slipped back to a scene he could not visualize. ''I had been back from France only two days. You arrived on the morning of the third day with four perfect red roses.''

''Four?''

''Mmm. One for each year you'd been in love with me.''

''Romantic devil,'' he muttered.

''Then you took me into the garden behind the house here. It's not much of a garden, really,'' Lavinia admitted, ''but it was a beautiful day, and the sun was shining brightly. You told me that…every day we had been apart, your heart had broken a little more, but that…you had been able to live with it because every day that passed also meant we were one day closer to the time we would be together.''

"I said that?" he whispered huskily.

"Yes. And then you went down on your knee and asked me to marry you."

"Which knee?"

"The right one."

Nicholas sank slowly down, bending his right knee to the floor. "I have no roses, Lavinia, and this is not the garden. But will you…marry me?"

Lavinia felt the sting of tears in her eyes. She had wanted so desperately for this to happen, for Nicholas to say, "Will you marry me?" so that she could put the past behind her and go forward once again. She had dreamed that she would hear the words. And yet, now that she had, they brought her hollow pleasure.

"No, Nicholas. I will not marry you. Not until I know that you are asking for the right reasons. I understand that you want to…protect me, and that it would be easier for you to do so if I were living under your roof—or you under mine. But marriage is for the rest of our lives, dearest," she said, willing him to understand. "Once this man is apprehended, you will still be married to me. And perhaps, knowing that you weren't ready to make the decision when you did, you will end up resenting me."

"No, that could never happen," Nicholas told her vehemently. "I want you, Lavinia. I love you!"

The words were out almost before he realized it, but as soon as he'd said them, Nicholas knew them to be the truth. He did love her. And he did want her to marry him. Not just for now, but for always. But his momentary hesitation had told Lavinia something else. She shook her head sadly. "You may say that you love me, Nicholas, but it is not in the way you did before, my darling. You cannot love me as totally as you did then. Not when so many other things are weighing on your mind, distracting you."

He shook his head. "I don't understand."

"Nicholas, when you fell in love with me all those years ago, it was because, on the day we met, you knew that there could be no one else in the world for you. Just as I realized that, even as I married another man, I could never love anyone but you. You felt no pressure to fall in love with me. No sense of decency, or obligation."

"My asking you to marry me now has nothing to do with obligation or decency," Nicholas retorted, the rich timbre of his voice striking an answering need in Lavinia's heart. "I'm asking you to marry me because I love you, damn it!"

"No, not totally," Lavinia replied with quiet emphasis. "Part of you is saying that you love me, but another part is telling you that you *should* love me. That you are obligated to love me because of what we meant to each other before your accident.

I don't want there to be any sense of obligation, Nicholas. I've had a taste of what it is to love you without reservation, and I cannot accept anything less. I would rather wait—or not marry you at all—than have you look back and feel you've made a mistake.''

Nicholas stared down at the floor, the silence lengthening between them. "I don't know what to say," he said finally. "I didn't expect you to say no.''

"And I haven't. Not exactly," Lavinia said with a return of her engaging smile. "I'm just saying…not yet. When all of this is over and you are not feeling pressured to do something because you feel you should, ask me again, Nicholas. And even if your memory has not returned, I will give you my answer. I promise.''

Nicholas rose and, taking her hands in his, drew her up beside him. "You are an incredible woman, Lavinia Duplesse. And a very sensible one.''

"Dear me, how unflattering." Lavinia strove for lightness in her voice, even as her tears trembled dangerously close to the surface. "I remember my governess once telling me that to be sensible was of more value to a lady than being beautiful. I remember disagreeing with her most heartily, even then.''

"Ah, but you have the benefit of being both, my dear," Nicholas said. "You are beautiful *and* sen-

sible. And the combination is most attractive." He
turned to go, and paused. "Lavinia?"

"Yes?"

"I will ask again."

She nodded. "I certainly hope so, my lord."

CHAPTER ELEVEN

KNOWING THAT LAVINIA and Martine were to stay in their own house only strengthened Nicholas's desire to find the man who had murdered Sullivan and Winchester. He knew he had to be in London for it was here he had sworn to carry out his threats. There was no reason for him to be anywhere else.

Nicholas saw Lavinia every day, stopping by her house frequently to ensure that she and Martine were all right. He took to attending most of the functions he was invited to, and every one that Lavinia was. He would not allow her or Martine to go anywhere on their own, and made sure that one of his own footmen was always present to escort the ladies wherever they went.

Lavinia, meanwhile, tried to keep herself busy. Part of her regretted having turned down Nicholas's proposal. She had waited so long to be with him again, and the knowledge that, by her own choice, she wasn't with him struck her as being somewhat absurd. On the other hand, she knew that it would not have been fair to Nicholas. Not now, when he had so many other things to worry about.

It went without saying that she had wanted to say yes, and for a moment, she almost had. But in her heart of hearts, she'd known what had prompted Nicholas to offer her marriage. Only when he came to her out of love would she accept his proposal. And if he didn't, well, that was something she would have to deal with. She told Lady Renton as much when they went driving the following afternoon.

"Livie, you are too noble for your own good," Caroline chided her. "The man asked you to marry him and you said no?"

"He only asked because he felt obligated to," Lavinia informed her friend, careful not to mention the protection aspect. "I think he feels guilty."

"And so he should after all the love and attention you have showered on him," Caroline observed. "Dear me, you should hear what some of the dowagers are saying. You're setting a very bad example for the rest of us, my dear."

"I beg your pardon?"

"Indeed. Your loyalty to Nicholas in spite of his continued loss of memory has earned you a great deal of respect, and some husbands of my acquaintance are advising their wives to take a page from your book.''

''Never!''

''Yes, indeed.''

''Not Lord Renton, I hope,'' Lavinia said sincerely.

''No, not William. He seems happy enough with the attention he gets,'' Caroline said fondly. ''But there are others who fare dreadfully in comparison to you, my dear.''

Lavinia started to laugh, a sound that quickly died at the approach of a familiar gentleman mounted on a big black horse. She stiffened and averted her gaze, praying that Caroline would drive on. Contrarily, Lady Renton, not knowing of Lavinia's aversion to the man, drew the carriage to a halt. ''Good afternoon, Lord Rushton,'' she greeted him cordially.

''Lady Renton, I have been watching you traverse the Park. I must say you handle the ribbons as well as any gentleman of my acquaintance, and better than many.''

''Your flattery is most appreciated, Lord Rushton,'' Caroline replied with an engaging grin. ''Perhaps you would be good enough to pass on your views to my husband the next time you see him. He is constantly telling me that I will never make a competent whip.''

Rushton smiled smoothly. "I shall be sure to."
He turned and swept Lavinia a courtly bow. "And
Lady Duplesse. Returned from the countryside so
soon? I had expected you to linger there longer."

Lavinia's voice was courteous, but distant. "The
countryside is delightful, Lord Rushton, but it does
not offer the scope of amusements to be found in
Town."

"I see. And was Miss Duplesse also eager to
return?"

Lavinia clenched her hands together in the folds
of her pelisse. "She is happy in either place. There
are still many youthful pleasures for her to enjoy
in the country."

"Yes, so I observed. I enjoyed seeing the two
of you in Canterbury that day. The cathedral
seemed to make a strong impression on Martine."

Lavinia's smile was cool. "*Miss Duplesse* is at
an impressionable age, my lord, and is often swept
away by a momentary fancy. She will grow out of
it in time."

"I hope she does not grow out of it too soon,
Lady Duplesse. She is a charming and spirited
creature. It would be a shame to see that enthusiasm curbed. But tell me, how do your own plans
go on?" he asked conversationally. "Have you
and Lord Longworth set the date yet?"

Her smile was chilly. "Not yet."

"Then I take it there has been no change in his condition?"

"None. In fact," Lavinia added, "I believe Lord Longworth fears there will not be any."

Rushton's eyes glowed with a strange intensity. "Then perhaps the two of you will not be getting married after all."

Lavinia stiffened. "That is between myself and my fiancé."

"But of course. Well, I shall detain you no longer. Enjoy your ride."

Doffing his hat, Rushton moved off, a lingering smile on his lips.

"Is it my imagination or do the two of you strike sparks?" Caroline observed drolly.

"It is not your imagination," Lavinia muttered. "In fact, were there loose tinder around, no doubt we should cause a blazing fire. I do not like that man above half!"

"That is quite obvious, my dear." Caroline whipped up the horses. "Unfortunately, it is also quite obvious that, regardless of your own feelings for the man, Lord Rushton is very interested in both you *and* Martine. Your Lord Longworth might do well to sit up and take notice!"

AT THE THEATRE the following evening, Martine peered excitedly through her quizzing glass at the rows of well-filled boxes lining the walls, while Lavinia sat quietly at her side and thought about her meeting with Lord Rushton. In truth, she was quite disturbed by it, just as she had been by every encounter they had had. It was almost as though he were toying with her. Her and Martine.

"Oh look, *maman*, is that not Lady Skifton down there?" Martine passed the quizzing glass to Lavinia. "The one in the purple velvet?"

Lavinia studied the box almost directly across from them and nodded. She didn't need a lorgnette to identify the woman; the lady's tremendous size gave her away. "Yes, I believe so."

Martine tittered. "The box does not look large enough to hold her and Lord Skifton both. However did she become so big, I wonder?"

Lavinia smiled. "Lady Skifton has a healthy appetite."

"But surely Lord Skifton cannot find her attractive any more."

"I don't know that he is overly concerned. They deal well enough together." Lavinia purposely did not mention that Lord Skifton had no need to deal with his wife, having kept a string of mistresses in a discreet house in Kensington for the last ten years.

Martine raised the glass to her eyes again and slowly swept the audience with her gaze. "Lady

Renton looks beautiful tonight. I see her there in the box next to… Oh!''

Lavinia heard the muffled exclamation, and turned to see that the girl's cheeks had flushed a bright pink. She was staring rather intently through the glass. ''What's wrong, Martine? Did you see a handsome gentleman looking at you?'' Lavinia teased.

''No, of course not.'' The girl's laugh was a touch too bright, and she quickly put down the glasses. ''When is Nicholas coming?''

At that moment, the velvet curtain behind them moved and Nicholas entered, along with Laura and Edward. ''Look who I bumped into downstairs.''

''But what a lovely surprise!'' Lavinia happily brushed Laura's cheek with her own. ''I did not know you were coming tonight.''

''Neither did I until this afternoon.'' Laura sat down in the seat next to her. ''Edward planned it as a bit of a surprise. Hello, Martine.''

''Good evening, Miss Beaufort, Mr. Kingsley.'' Martine's face lit up as she turned to greet Nicholas. ''Oh, Nicholas, this is so exciting. Thank you so very much for inviting me.''

''It was my pleasure.'' Nicholas and Edward sat down in the seats directly behind their ladies. ''I thought it might be an enjoyable performance. I understand Kean is not one to disappoint his audiences.''

Lavinia turned and smiled into Nicholas's eyes. ''You have made her night,'' she whispered.

Nicholas bent forward slightly and pressed his lips to the curve of Lavinia's bare neck as the lights began to dim. ''Just as you have made mine, dear lady. You look beautiful.''

Lavinia blushed and quickly turned around, aware that the curtain was rising.

As expected, Kean gave a brilliant performance. Martine was entranced, as much by the ugly actor's rich speaking voice as she was by his amazing stage presence. After a particularly stirring scene in the second half, Nicholas leaned forward. ''Would you like me to fetch some lemonade?''

Lavinia turned gratefully. ''Oh, yes, that would be most appreciated, Nicholas. Thank you.''

''I'll come with you, shall I?'' Edward offered. ''More ladies here than you can carry drinks for, I'm afraid.''

Downstairs, Edward and Nicholas made their way through the crowd of bejewelled matrons, dazzling dandies and bored theatre-goers who came as much to be seen themselves as for seeing the play. Nicholas nodded to some acquaintances and glanced around.

"Quite the crowd, eh, Nicholas?" Edward observed drily.

"Indeed. Is it always thus?"

"Pretty much so, though Kean's performances do tend to pack them in more than usual."

Nicholas nodded, and the two men jostled their way closer to the area where lemonade was being served. It was while he was waiting that he heard a group of gentlemen somewhere behind him discussing the entertainment.

"Well, of course, it's all a play on good versus evil. And if that's the case, we know who has to win," one voice observed.

"Yes, but the hero is such a lacklustre character," another said critically. "Indeed, I almost wish the villain would triumph, even though you know the fellow's going to die at the end."

"Personally, I've always found villains to be much more colourful figures," a third voice said mockingly. "In fact, I've often wondered whether it isn't better to live a villain than to die a hero."

Nicholas froze. *Better to live a villain than to die a hero.* Those words. Why did they seem so...familiar? And that voice?

He whipped around, suddenly aware that his vision was blurring. His mind was being inundated with names, with faces.

Better to die a hero than to live a coward. No,

not a statement, he realized, shaking his head, try-ing to clear the mists that were closing in around him. A question.

Is it more noble to die a hero or to live a cow-ard?

A question put to him by—

Nicholas gasped, and abruptly felt sweat break-ing out on his forehead. In one blinding moment it all came back—everything a murderer's bullet had wiped from his mind that fateful night in France. His family, his work, Lavinia, his life—all were brought rushing back by a single question, a question casually overheard in the midst of a crowded theatre lobby.

A question put to him by the very man who had shot him from his horse and left him in the road to die!

"*MAMAN*, WHERE HAS Nicholas gone?" Martine enquired.

"To get some lemonade for us." Lavinia turned and smiled at her stepdaughter. "Are you thirsty?"

"Yes, very much. May I...go and look for him?"

"I don't know if that is a good idea, Martine. The lobby is no doubt extremely crowded."

Martine's eyes were unusually bright. "Please, *maman,* it will be all right. Nicholas will be there."

Lavinia glanced at Laura. "What do you think?"

"I don't see that she will come to any harm. As she says, Nicholas and Edward are both downstairs."

Lavinia nodded. "All right then, Martine, but make sure you find them right away and stay with them until they return."

"Yes, *maman*."

When Martine had gone, Lavinia started to laugh. "Do you know, Laura, I remember my first evening at the theatre. I was so excited, I couldn't sleep the whole night before."

"What did you see?"

"I've no idea," Lavinia admitted. "I was so busy watching the people in the audience that I scarcely paid five minutes attention to what was happening on stage."

The curtain twitched a few minutes later and Edward reappeared. "Did I miss anything?"

Laura shook her head, accepting the glass of lemonade he handed her. "Not really."

Lavinia smiled, and waited for Nicholas and Martine to enter. When they did not, she frowned. "Edward, are Nicholas and Martine not with you?"

"No, I lost track of Nicholas when I went up to

get the refreshments. I thought perhaps he'd already come back. Has he not returned?''

''No. Nor has Martine. Did you see her downstairs?''

Edward looked at her sharply. ''She came down? When?''

''A little while ago. She went to look for you and Nicholas. And now neither of them are here,'' Lavinia replied, panic beginning to tinge her voice. ''Edward, where are they?''

He was already out of his seat. ''Calm yourself, Lavinia. I'll go back down and find them. Don't either of you leave this box.''

Edward disappeared through the curtain, leaving Lavinia to look after him nervously. ''Laura, what could have happened to them?''

''You don't know that anything has happened to them, Lavinia,'' Laura replied reassuringly. ''It was crowded downstairs. Martine may have become disoriented when she was looking for Nicholas.''

''But where did Nicholas go? Why didn't he tell Edward he was coming back up here, if that's what he was planning to do?''

Lavinia stood up. Laura stared at her. ''Lavinia, where are you going?''

''To look for them.''

''But Edward told us—''

"I know what Edward told us, but I'm worried. I can't just sit here and wait."

"Oh, all right. But I'm coming, too," Laura said.

"No, you stay here in case Martine returns. She'll be worried if she comes back and there is no one here. You can just tell her that I...had to get a breath of fresh air."

Grudgingly, Laura sat down, her face clearly worried. "You *will* hurry back?"

"Just as soon as I find them."

Lavinia turned and quit the box, making her way down to the crowded lobby. Dear Lord, how was she to find anyone in this throng? She anxiously scanned the faces of the people below, but Martine was nowhere to be seen. Nor was Nicholas.

"Lady Duplesse, you look a trifle upset. Could I be of some assistance?"

Lavinia turned and found herself looking into Lord Havermere's smiling, urbane face. "Oh, Lord Havermere, I was just...looking for my stepdaughter. Have you seen her, by any chance?"

"Yes, as a matter of fact, I have. I saw her talking to Lord Rushton just outside the theatre."

"Rushton!" The knot of fear in Lavinia's stomach tightened. "But what were they doing outside?"

"I don't know. Perhaps I could show you where I last saw them."

Lavinia quickly scanned the crowded lobby once more. It was getting even worse now. The performance was over and people were beginning to pour from the interior. In a few minutes she wouldn't be able to find anyone. "Yes, all right," she agreed reluctantly.

With Havermere clearing the way, she made her way outside, to where a crowd was already milling about. The street was filled to overflowing with carriages, both private and for hire. Lavinia struggled to see around the hordes of people jostling for position.

"Down here a little, I think, Lady Duplesse," Havermere said. "I believe I just caught a glimpse of Lord Rushton's coat."

By now Lavinia's fears had intensified. They were farther away from the theatre. It was darker here, and there were not so many people around.

"Lord Havermere, perhaps I should—" She got no further. Finding herself beside a closed carriage, she suddenly felt a large hand close over her mouth as her arms were grabbed and pinned behind her back. The door of the carriage opened and she was shoved unceremoniously inside. Havermere shouted something to the coachman and then sprang in behind her, slamming the door.

They set off so quickly that Lavinia was thrown against him. She felt his hands close around her arms. Before she had a chance to say anything, Havermere had extracted a length of cord from under the seat and was tying it securely around her wrists.

"What are you doing?" Lavinia demanded. "Let me out this instant or I shall scream!"

"You're not in a position to be ordering anyone about, my dear Lady Duplesse," Havermere said smoothly. "And I wouldn't bother to scream. At the moment, I have the upper hand and you are going to do exactly as I tell you."

"What do you mean? Why should I do anything you tell me to?"

"Because if you don't, I guarantee you will not see your precious Martine alive again."

NICHOLAS OPENED HIS EYES to find himself lying face down on the floor. He groaned and gingerly lifted a hand to the lump on the back of his head. He hadn't even seen it coming. He'd been so intent on following Havermere that he hadn't noticed the man hiding behind the curtain.

Slowly, Nicholas eased himself into a sitting position and waited for the room to stop spinning. He was obviously still in the theatre, judging from the assortment of stage props stacked around him. This must have been where the man deposited him after knocking him out.

Nicholas remembered it all now—the reason he'd gone to France, the inn he'd stayed at; ambushing the carriage carrying Leclerc and the other Englishman. And the man on the black horse who had ridden up through the darkness and shot him— a man whose face he had only glimpsed through shadows—but whose voice he would remember until the day he died.

Havermere. Havermere was the one who had shot him and left him there in the ditch to die. It was Havermere who had taunted him with the very words that had exposed him tonight, and it was probably he who had cold-bloodedly killed Winchester and Sullivan. Not Rushton, as Nicholas had begun to suspect, but Rushton's good friend Lord Havermere, the man who had questioned him so closely about Lavinia...

Lavinia! He remembered her, too. Everything about her. The love and the compassion they had felt for one another. The years of longing when they'd lived apart. His good friend Devon Marwood, risking his life to bring her out of France. Their reunion when she had finally returned to England. Even the proposal she had had to tell him about only a few days ago.

He remembered it all. And now that he had, it

was time to put things right. To take care of things properly. But first, he had to get back to the box. Lavinia was probably beside herself with worry. He'd have to warn them all.

The moment he stepped out of the room however, Nicholas knew it wasn't going to be that easy. He must have been unconscious longer than he'd thought.

The theatre was in complete darkness, the doors locked and barred. There wasn't a soul in the place.

LAVINIA HAD NO IDEA where Havermere was taking her. All of the carriage windows were covered. But that really didn't matter at the moment. All that mattered was that he had Martine, and that he would not hesitate to kill her if he thought it necessary.

"Why?" Lavinia asked quietly. "Why are you doing this? What have Martine and I done to you?"

"The two of you have done nothing," Havermere replied. "I simply intend to use you to facilitate my next...accident."

"Accident?"

"Yes. Lord Sullivan met with a most unfortunate one when he was out hunting. And then there was poor Winchester, viciously set upon on his way home after a pleasant evening of gambling.

Such a pity, but—'' Havermere grinned evilly ''—accidents will happen.''

Stark, black fear settled in the pit of Lavinia's stomach, stopping the breath in her throat. Havermere was the murderer! It was Havermere who had shot Nicholas that night in France and left him for dead, just as it was Havermere who had arranged poor Lord Winchester's murder and now, by the sounds of it, Lord Sullivan's.

''Why so silent all of a sudden, Lavinia?'' Havermere asked, breaking into her thoughts. ''Nothing to say?''

She shivered. ''How can anyone be so evil?''

''My dear Lavinia, this is war, and war is business. A business fought between countries.''

''But you're dealing with innocent peoples' lives!''

''An expendable commodity.'' Havermere's voice was totally expressionless. ''Besides, Winchester and Sullivan were hardly innocent. They knew what they were getting into when they went into the service. Just as François did.''

Lavinia felt a wave of revulsion and nausea. ''You killed my husband.''

''Actually, no.'' Havermere studied his smooth leather gloves impassively. ''I did not kill your husband. I merely gave the order that he be killed. The man Longworth shot on that country road in

France did the actual work for me. Speaking of which, I nearly forgot about that accident—another one of mine. Two gentlemen and a cleric shot dead in a midnight robbery on a deserted country road. Quite original, I thought. Pity I slipped up, though," Havermere remarked as though he were discussing the state of the weather.

"You're the one!" Lavinia flung the words at him, her suspicions confirmed. "You're the one who shot Nicholas and left him to die."

Havermere smiled coldly. "Yes, most negligent on my part. I don't usually leave loose ends. They have a nasty way of turning up again. That's why I put a bullet in his head as well as his side, or so I thought. Fortunately, Nicholas hasn't been able to do me any harm. He was very lucky to have suffered that memory loss. Otherwise I would have had to kill him right away. Perhaps I should have done so regardless. It would have saved me all this bother now, though I admit it's been rather amusing to watch him stumbling around Town, acting like a backward schoolboy."

"You disgust me!" Lavinia whispered in a voice resonant with hatred.

"Really. Then I take it you would not welcome my presence as a husband."

Lavinia blanched. "About as much as I would

welcome the devil's! Where is Martine?'' she demanded in a choked voice.

''Oh, you needn't worry, she is quite safe. Rushton told her—''

''Rushton! What has Rushton to do with this?'' Lavinia demanded.

''Quite a lot, actually. I doubt I would have been able to get out of France had he not arranged for the boat to meet me at Calais.''

''Rushton…helped you? But why?''

''Because while his interest in Napoleon's cause was not the same as mine, it was sufficient to sway his loyalties away from England. His mother was just one of many French aristocrats who had her family's lands and properties confiscated. Rushton hoped that with the success of Bonaparte, he would have a chance at reclaiming those lands. Sadly, it would appear now that such is not to be the case.''

''What has Rushton done with Martine?''

''Oh, you needn't worry. He hasn't hurt her. He simply told her that he was escorting her to Rose Cottage as per your instructions.''

''*My* instructions! And she believed him?''

''She would have no reason not to. I understand the two of them have become quite close over the last little while.'' Havermere chuckled unpleasantly. ''She even sneaked out of the theatre to meet him this evening. And of course, Rushton would have no wish to hurt his future bride.''

''His *bride?* Don't be ridiculous, I would never allow Martine to marry Lord Rushton!''

''I wouldn't sound so sure if I were you, my dear.'' Havermere was clearly unconcerned. ''She is of marriageable age, and Rushton finds her quite charming. She is young, yes, and terribly naive, but she will learn.'' His eyes glowed as he turned to look at her. ''Just as you could learn to love me.''

Lavinia shuddered. ''I could no more learn to love you than I could a toad!''

The smile abruptly faded from Havermere's face, to be replaced by an ugly, menacing sneer. ''That will be quite enough. I have been very tolerant with you thus far, Lavinia, but there is nothing to say that my charity has to continue. I am quite capable of making your death look as accidental as Sullivan's.''

Lavinia swallowed. ''Why have you kidnapped me?''

''Kidnapped? I have not kidnapped you, my dear. I am merely providing a ride back to the country for you. To Rose Cottage.''

''Then what is it you want?''

''What I want is quite simple.'' The mien of the sophisticated gentleman was back in place. ''You will write a letter to Lord Longworth telling him that you and Martine have returned to the house in Kent for a few days because you believe you know the identity of the killer and now fear for your safety in London. To that end, you will also ask him to come and see you as soon as possible.''

"So that you can kill him there?"

"Not at all," Havermere informed her in the tone of a tutor to his pupil. "I don't intend that he will ever reach Kent. You see, there will be an unfortunate incident with a footpad on the road. And this time, poor Lord Longworth will not survive.''

"You cannot mean this!"

"Ah, but I do, my dear. I have been patient long enough, but now I have reason to believe that Longworth suspects who I am. Rushton discovered him following me in the theatre this evening. And being that you also know, I cannot risk your getting together with him again. As soon as we reach our first stop, you will write the letter for me so that it can be delivered to your precious fiancé.''

"No!"

He continued as if she hadn't spoken. "You will also write one to your friend Miss Beaufort, telling her that everything is fine and that you and Martine have decided to return to Kent. After all, she was most taken with the house, as I recall Martine telling Rushton. She will certainly not find it strange that you have returned. Then we will continue down to Rose Cottage, where Martine is anxiously awaiting your arrival. She will be delighted to see that I have brought her mama to her.''

''I will tell her exactly what you and Rushton have done,'' Lavinia said in a low voice.

''On the contrary, you will tell her nothing,'' Havermere said coldly. ''Because if you do, it will not only be Lord Longworth who meets with an accident, but the charming Miss Beaufort, as well.''

''Dear God! Laura!''

''Yes, it is always so helpful when people have friends.''

''But she has nothing to do with this! Or with you!''

''Indirectly, she has,'' Havermere tossed back. ''She will be marrying Edward Kingsley, a rather exceptional British agent, and one who has caused me no end of irritation. That is reason enough to kill her—if you force me to.''

Lavinia fought to stem the rising tide of nausea. ''You cannot possibly get away with this. People will come looking. Edward will—''

''Kingsley will do nothing, because after I take care of Lord Longworth tonight, I will return to London and tell Mr. Kingsley that the two of you are enjoying a lover's rendezvous. Hence, there will be no reason for him to be suspicious. And, after all, he would hardly wish to disturb a pair of lovers, would he?''

"Edward won't believe you."

"He will, at first. But he'll be dead before he has time to figure it out and tell anyone else."

"You're mad!" Lavinia gasped.

"Not in the least. In fact, I am extremely sane. And the idea is, I think, quite a good one."

"You seem to have forgotten one thing."

"Oh?"

"What about me?" Lavinia asked quietly. "I know all about your plans. Do you think I will sit by and watch you get away with them?"

"Not for a moment," Havermere said with an engaging smile. "Once Nicholas is taken care of, there will be an unfortunate fire at Rose Cottage. Luckily, Rushton will be in the area and manage to save poor Martine, thereby ensuring her devotion to him. But I'm afraid he will not be able to reach her stepmother's room in time. A most tragic loss.''

Lavinia swallowed again, closing her eyes against the face of a madman. He had it all planned. "And the others?" she asked in a strangled voice.

"They will be dealt with in my own time and in my own way. Now, my dear, I suggest you start thinking about what you are going to say in the letter to your dear fiancé. Because once we reach our first stop, you will have a very short time to write it before my man arrives to take it back to London.''

''I won't do it.'' Lavinia returned his steady regard. ''I will not lure Nicholas to his death.''

''Then you condemn Martine to hers,'' Havermere said emotionlessly. ''Rushton will get over it. I only promised Martine to him as a reward for his services. And it really doesn't matter, because Longworth will die anyway. But if you agree, Lavinia, you can at least know that Martine will live. Is it not better to know that she will survive, rather than see *everyone* dispatched?''

Lavinia turned away from the repulsive sight of his face, horrified by the choices he had given her, but knowing deep in her heart that he had given her no choice at all.

CHAPTER TWELVE

THE FIRST PLACE Nicholas went after leaving the theatre was to Lavinia's house. He wasn't surprised to find that neither she nor Martine were there. Upon questioning Lavinia's maid, he discovered that neither lady had returned home from the theatre.

Thankfully, he was more successful at his second stop. "Nicholas! Where the hell have you been?" Edward demanded after ushering his friend inside. "I searched everywhere in that damn theatre for you."

"Unfortunately, you forgot the prop room," Nicholas informed him ruefully. "Seems the murderer was correct in assuming it would be a safe hiding-place for me. But never mind that. Where's Lavinia?"

"I don't know. After I lost track of you downstairs, I went back to the box, assuming you'd already gone up. Lavinia and Laura were there, but you weren't."

"Where was Martine?"

"Apparently, she'd gone to look for you. I told the ladies I was going back down and ordered them to stay put. But when I returned, Lavinia was gone and Laura was having fits!"

"And Lavinia never came back?"

"Neither of them did. When I couldn't find you in the theatre, I left to take Laura home, hoping you would eventually turn up here. If you hadn't appeared within the next fifteen minutes, I was on my way to Osborne."

"It wouldn't have made any difference. He's already got both of them."

"Who?"

"Havermere. It's been Havermere all along. Havermere was the man who shot me in France."

"But how do you—" Edward gasped. "Good Lord, your memory's come back?"

"With stunning clarity."

"But how? When?"

"I overheard Havermere and Rushton talking at the theatre earlier. Something Havermere said took me back to that night, and that's when it all came flooding in, like a huge dam breaking. I began to remember faces, names. And I remembered his voice. That's when I realized that Havermere was the man who'd shot me."

"What happened then?"

"I started to follow him, but I was hit from behind."

"Bloody hell, when I think we had him right in the palm of our hand and let him slip away."

"I know, my friend, I know. And it sickens me to think that he has Lavinia and Martine."

"So what now?"

"I shall go to see Lord Osborne and let him know what's happened. Then we wait."

"What? Sit back and do nothing? Are you mad?"

"I'm afraid we don't have much choice," Nicholas said grimly. "As much as I would like to tear London apart brick by brick searching for them, it would be a complete waste of time. Havermere could be hiding them almost anywhere. I'm afraid we're going to have to wait for him to make the first move."

"What about your memory? Are you going to tell anyone?"

"No!" Nicholas all but shouted the word. "As far as everyone else is concerned, nothing has changed. Only you and Osborne will know differently. Lavinia's and Martine's lives may very well depend on it."

"SO IT WAS HAVERMERE all along." Lord Osborne slammed his fist down on the desk in his library, where Nicholas had been ushered by a sleepy servant. "Damn! When I think of the times we could have had him."

"It doesn't matter now, my lord," Nicholas said. "What matters is that he has Lavinia and Martine, and that he will use them to get to me."

"Yes, you're right, of course. What do you want me to do?"

"Nothing, for the moment. I'm afraid we're totally at Havermere's mercy," Nicholas admitted. "We don't know where he's hiding the ladies or precisely what he intends to do. My guess is he will contact us as soon as he's ready. And the moment he does, we must be prepared to move."

The manner of contact did not turn out precisely as Nicholas had expected, however. A few hours later, a letter was delivered to the back kitchen of Nicholas's house by a young lad who disappeared into the night the moment he left it.

"Shall I give chase, sir?" his butler offered, handing Nicholas the missive.

Nicholas shook his head. "No. I doubt the boy will be able to tell us anything." Havermere was far too clever to be exposed so easily.

Nicholas quickly broke the seal. His hand began to tremble as he recognized Lavinia's elegant writing.

My dearest Nicholas,

Pray forgive my hasty departure from the the-atre, but I thought it best that Martine and I leave London as soon as possible. I now know the identity of the man who shot you, and realize that the safest place for us is at Rose Cottage. Please come as soon as you can. We only have a mere few hours before he finds us.

Yours,
Lavinia

Nicholas read the letter twice over before he saw it: *...have a mere few hours...*

He closed his eyes, fighting down a wave of intense anger. *Havermere.* Havermere was using Lavinia to lure him to Rose Cottage. Her carefully worded letter was a warning that he would be walking into a trap.

Nicholas crushed the letter into a ball. Very well, the game was in motion; his opponent had made the first move. Now it was up to Nicholas to play along until he got the opportunity to take the upper hand. And he fully intended to do so, as quickly and as quietly as possible. But if anything were to happen to Lavinia or Martine in the mean-

time, nothing on earth would stop him from bringing the game to a swift and brutal conclusion.
Nothing!

"IT'S A TRAP," Edward said when he'd finished
reading the letter. "He's obviously going to be
waiting for you at the cottage."

Nicholas nodded. "Of course. And he's using
Lavinia as bait."

"Do you think she and Martine are even there?"

Nicholas shrugged. "I don't know. The problem
is, I can't afford to take any chances until I know
for sure. I have to play along."

Edward put the letter on the table. "When are
you leaving?"

"As soon as I've seen Osborne. I expect he will
offer to provide me with backup if I want it."

"And do you?"

Nicholas grinned. "I was thinking about taking
along the best man I know. Are you available?"

Edward smiled in a conspiratorial fashion. "Just
try to stop me."

AS SOON AS HE'D BEEN to see Lord Osborne, Nicholas set out. He was far too agitated to wait until
dawn. The sooner he reached Rose Cottage, the
sooner he could see to Martine's and Lavinia's
safety.

At the thought of the beautiful and brave woman

who had risked so much to see him well again, Nicholas offered up a silent prayer for her safety. Through everything that had happened, Lavinia had stuck with him, encouraging him, loving him. And now it was his turn to show Lavinia how deeply he cared. Because long before his memory had returned, Nicholas knew that he had fallen totally and quite hopelessly in love with Lavinia Duplesse—again.

Rounding a bend in the road, he suddenly came upon the sight of a carriage stopped dead in the middle of the road. The horses were still hitched, but the back wheel was badly smashed. Nicholas reined in, his dark eyebrows slanting in a frown. The door to the carriage was thrown open, yet there did not appear to be anyone within. Spilling out over the steps was a cloak. A lady's cloak.

Lavinia's cloak!

Nicholas dismounted and cautiously approached the carriage. His gaze intent on the vehicle, he did not at first notice the shadowy figure on horseback standing just inside the trees. It wasn't until he heard the familiar sound of a pistol being cocked that he realized he had stumbled into his trap a little sooner than expected.

"So, my friend, I find you on a deserted stretch of road again."

Nicholas swallowed, and drawing on whatever

acting skills he possessed, turned around and looked in the direction of the horseman, feigning surprise. "Who goes there?"

"Do you not recognize me, Nicholas?"

"Havermere? Is that you? For God's sake, man, this is no time to be playing games. There's been an accident here."

"So it would appear."

Nicholas turned away from Havermere and started walking towards the carriage. With every step he half expected to feel the thud of a bullet in his back. But there was nothing else he could do. If he reached for his pistol, Havermere would shoot him down. He had to pretend that he was not aware of the danger. His life—and Lavinia's—depended on his acting totally believable. "Will you not lend me a hand?"

"I hardly think it necessary. There don't appear to be any passengers within."

"But surely that is a lady's cloak."

"It may well be. But tell me, Nicholas, what are you doing out on the road so late?"

"I am on my way to see Lavinia." Nicholas threw the words back over his shoulder. "She sent me a letter asking me to come."

"And being the dutiful fiancé, you came at once, eh?"

"Do you find it so strange that I would wish to be with her?"

Havermere appeared to be enjoying himself. "Not at all. She is a beautiful woman. In fact, what would you say were I to tell you that I was thinking of asking Lavinia for her hand in marriage?"

Nicholas was thankful for the darkness, which hid his rage. "I would wonder why you were wasting your time, when you know the lady is already betrothed to me."

"Yes, but if you were to leave again... unexpectedly, Lavinia would be left all alone once more."

"Fortunately, I do not intend to leave."

The wind suddenly picked up. Nicholas heard a faint rustling in the grass. "But come, Havermere, the middle of the night is hardly the time to be discussing marriage possibilities."

"No, Nicholas, indeed it is not, and I confess this polite social chit-chat is beginning to bore me. I would have liked it better had you regained your memory. There is really no sport in killing a man who doesn't even know why he is going to die."

Nicholas quickly calculated the distance between himself and the carriage. No more than two steps. "What are you talking about?"

"Oh, really, Nicholas, this is growing quite tedious. Do you not know that it was I who shot you in France that night?''

''You! But—''

''Throw down your weapon, Havermere!'' Edward's voice reverberated through the darkness like a pistol shot.

Havermere whirled round in the saddle. ''What the—''

In the split second Havermere's attention was diverted, Nicholas threw himself under the carriage. He heard Havermere's muffled oath, and then the sound of a shot. The bullet landed in the dirt only inches from where he lay. But it was the only shot Havermere was to get. Cocking his own pistol, Nicholas rolled out from under the carriage and, getting to his feet on the other side, took aim and fired.

The bullet hit Havermere in the upper body, knocking him out of the saddle. Nicholas watched his adversary land heavily on the dirt road, and then tensed as the injured man raised his hand, still clutching his pistol.

''I wouldn't do that if I were you,'' Edward warned in a silken voice. He emerged from the bushes just behind Havermere's horse, his own weapon aimed directly at the scoundrel's chest. ''I wouldn't think twice about shooting a cold-blooded murderer like you.''

Havermere's face contorted with anger and pain. "Kingsley! By God, I should have killed you when I had the chance. You've caused me nothing but trouble."

"And very glad I am to hear it." Edward kicked Havermere's pistol away with his foot. "Now, my lord, face down on the road, if you don't mind. Nice piece of shooting, Nicholas."

"Thank you." Nicholas looked up at the sound of a second carriage arriving. The door opened and Lord Osborne stepped down, flanked by two armed guards, their pistols trained on the man lying in the road.

"So, Havermere, it ends like this." Osborne stared down at the wounded man in disgust. "You should have known better than to take on my two best men."

By now, Havermere was saying very little, but Nicholas wasn't finished with him. "Where are they, my lord?"

Havermere's lips pulled back in a malevolent smile. "Go to hell!"

"On the contrary, hell is more likely somewhere you will be going if you don't answer my question in the next three seconds." Nicholas cocked his pistol and placed the end of the barrel against Havermere's temple. "Like Kingsley said, it would give me great pleasure to avenge François's murder right here and now, not to mention Baker's, Winchester's and God knows how many others'. Now, I shall ask you one last time. Where are they!"

Havermere laughed, but it was little more than a rasp. "They're where I told you they would be. At the cottage."

Nicholas gave him a cold, hard look. "They had better be, Havermere. And for your sake, they had better both be safe, or you're going to wish my first bullet had killed you right off."

Without waiting to hear anything more, Nicholas swung up into the saddle and headed in the direction of Rose Cottage. There was only one thought in his mind now—to find Lavinia and Martine as soon as possible. And if Havermere had done anything to harm them, by God, he'd tear him apart with his bare hands!

NICHOLAS SAW A FAINT light emanating from the drawing-room window as soon as the cottage came into view. He also saw a carriage waiting in the drive, and abruptly drew his stallion to a halt.

Someone other than Lavinia and Martine was inside the house!

Nicholas swore softly under his breath. He hadn't expected Havermere to post a guard. Obviously, he was working in league with someone—

and Nicholas had a pretty strong suspicion as to who that person might be.

He pulled the pistol from his belt and silently slid out of the saddle. Creeping through the darkness like an avenging angel, he made his way round to the back of the cottage and cautiously peered in through the leaded window. What he saw made his mouth narrow into a tight, angry line.

Lavinia was sitting on a chair with her wrists and ankles bound. Seated a few feet away, with his back to the window and a pistol held loosely in his hand, was Rushton.

Nicholas crouched back down below the window and struggled to contain his anger. *Rushton.* He might have known that bastard would be in on this. No wonder he'd been hanging around Martine and asking questions, trying to discover the extent of Nicholas's injuries. No wonder he and Havermere had appeared to be such good friends.

Nicholas frowned, anger hardening his features into a stony mask. He was tempted to burst into the room and open fire, but he knew he couldn't risk it. Lavinia might be wounded in the exchange. No, he would have to remain calm and think the situation through—luckily, something that took only minutes to do. Rushton might have Lavinia, but Martine was nowhere in sight. Which meant that he had probably locked her upstairs in her room, inadvertently giving Nicholas the advantage he needed.

Tucking the pistol securely into his belt, Nicholas approached the rose-draped trellis that covered the back of the cottage. Finding it sturdy enough to hold his weight, he quickly began to climb. In a matter of minutes he had reached the window to Martine's room, and seconds later had eased open the casement and slipped quietly inside.

"Nicholas!" Martine flung herself into his arms, sobbing.

Nicholas gathered the trembling girl to him and held her close. "Hush, Martine, hush. Everything is going to be all right now."

"Oh, Nicholas, I was so afraid," she whispered tearfully against his jacket. "Lord Rushton...forced me to get into the carriage at the theatre. He—he said that...*maman* was coming, and that we were to...wait for her here. But I haven't seen her. Is *maman* here, Nicholas? Is she all right?"

"Lavinia is downstairs in the drawing-room, Martine, and she's all right, but—"

"But...Lord Rushton is...with her?"

Nicholas sighed. "Yes, and I'm going to need your help in getting her away. We're going to have to create a diversion."

Martine sniffed again, then wiped away her

tears. She nodded, suddenly looking very grown-up indeed. "Tell me what you want me to do, Nicholas."

IN THE DRAWING-ROOM below, Lavinia sat in the chair and stared at the floor in front of her. She tried not to think about what might have happened to Nicholas. It seemed an eternity since she had last seen him. Where was he? Was he all right? Had he seen and understood the message hidden in her letter?

"I am going to marry her, you know," Rushton said, suddenly breaking into Lavinia's thoughts. "For all your warning me away from Martine, I will have her in the end. You can't stop me now."

Lavinia kept her eyes on the floor, unwilling to look at him. "She will never agree to marry you. I shall tell her what kind of monster you really are, and she will never go to you."

But Rushton only laughed softly. "No, Lavinia, not this time. You won't have a chance to say anything to her. And she won't hate me. She will be eternally grateful to me for having saved her life, even though I won't be able to save yours when this place goes up in— What the hell?" Rushton broke off at the sound of a loud crash, followed by a high-pitched scream.

Lavinia looked towards the stairs in horror. "Martine!"

Rushton was already moving. He grabbed the oil lamp from the table, and ignoring Lavinia's cries, raised his pistol and made for the stairs.

In the bedroom above, Nicholas waited patiently behind the door. "Lie perfectly still, Martine," he whispered to the girl who lay stretched out on the floor as if unconscious. "We have to make Lord Rushton believe that you've been injured."

It wasn't an unlikely conclusion, given the way the shattered fragments of the cheval-glass lay all around her—the mirror Nicholas had smashed with one good blow from the warming pan and then sent crashing to the floor.

Nicholas heard the sound of Rushton's footsteps on the stairs and pressed his body back against the wall, holding the barrel of his pistol tightly in his hand. He would have only one chance at this.

Abruptly, the door flew open. Rushton paused on the threshold of the room and stared down at the girl lying seemingly unconscious on the floor.

Nicholas tensed, his fingers clenching the pistol. As Rushton moved forward, he stepped out from behind the door and brought the butt of the weapon down hard on the back of Rushton's head. The man groaned and crumpled limply to the floor, unconscious.

Nicholas expelled the breath he hadn't even realized he'd been holding, and then dropped his pistol on the bed. It was over.

"Nicholas?" Martine whispered, her voice muffled against the floor. "Can I get up now?"

"Yes, Martine, you can." He carefully lifted the girl out of the wreckage of broken glass and sat her down on the bed. "Lord Rushton won't be troubling us any more."

"Is *maman* all right?" She asked in a whisper.

"That's what I intend to find out as soon as I take care of our friend here."

Nicholas quickly secured Rushton's ankles and wrists, using strong lengths of cotton torn from the sheets on Martine's bed. Nodding in satisfaction, he returned to Martine, still sitting on the bed, and handed her his pistol. "Now, I need you to stay here and guard our prisoner for a few minutes while I see to Lavinia. Can you do that, Martine?"

She nodded, a fierce look on her face. "I shall be fine, Nicholas. If Lord Rushton moves, I shall shoot him!"

"Dear me, you needn't go quite that far," Nicholas murmured with a smile as he bent to pick up Rushton's weapon. "Just keep the pistol trained on him. He won't be coming round for a while yet, and when he does, he certainly won't be going anywhere." Nicholas gave Martine a reassuring wink. "You just watch him for me, and I'll be back in a matter of minutes."

LAVINIA HEARD THE SOUND of footsteps coming down the stairs and strained her eyes towards the door. She held her breath as the light from the lamp drew closer. "Martine?" she whispered fearfully.

But it wasn't her stepdaughter who appeared on the threshold of the room and then strode forward, his face set in rigid lines as he looked down at the woman he loved. "Lavinia!"

"Nicholas? Oh, dear God, Nicholas, you're safe!" Lavinia cried, the feeling of relief so strong it nearly made her swoon. "But what happened? Where is Martine? I heard the crash—"

"Martine is safe, my darling. It was just a trick to lure Rushton away from you. He is safely bound and gagged upstairs." Nicholas swiftly untied the ropes restraining her, aware that his hands were shaking. "Thanks to your letter, I realized that I would be walking into a trap. As a result, Edward and I planned our own midnight ambush. Havermere is now in Osborne's custody and on his way back to London."

"Nicholas!" It was the only word Lavinia uttered before she fell into Nicholas's open arms and felt herself being crushed against his heart. She clung to him, drawing on his strength, relishing the closeness of his strong, hard body. "I was so afraid for you, Nicholas."

"I know, darling, I know, but it's all right now," he murmured huskily against her hair, holding her as though he would never let her go. "Everything's going to be all right. We're safe now, and we're going to stay that way. Because I'm never going away again, do you hear, Lavinia?" Nicholas whispered fervently. "I am never, ever going to leave you again!"

WHEN LAVINIA CAME downstairs the following morning, her cheeks were pale, but otherwise her face bore little evidence of the strain of the previous day and night. And what a night it had been. Shortly after she had been freed, Edward and one of Osborne's men had unexpectedly arrived at the cottage, to make sure that everything was all right. Rushton had been taken away, and Edward had returned to London, anxious to comfort an overwrought Laura. Martine had gone to bed, exhausted, and was, it seemed, still sleeping peacefully.

"Thank God she is young and resilient," Lavinia said now as she and Nicholas stood quietly by the window, looking out into the peaceful garden. "She will forget all about this, just as she did about François's death."

Nicholas heard Lavinia's heavy sigh and turned to regard her in silence. In the demure sprigged-muslin gown, and with her hair caught back in a loose cluster of curls, she barely looked older than Martine. Only the nervous fluttering of her hands betrayed her lingering memories of the frightening events.

"Lavinia, I wonder if you might like to join me for a walk in the garden."

Lavinia glanced up at him in surprise. "What...now?"

"Why not?" Taking her hand, he opened the French doors that led onto the terrace and guided her towards the sunny garden. "Can you think of a better time?"

Lavinia frowned as he led her outside to the very bench where they had sat just a few nights ago. "A better time for what?" She watched in confusion as Nicholas picked up a pair of garden shears. "Nicholas, what are you doing?"

"I'm trying to remember what you told me the other day. Now, sit there and don't say a word."

Nicholas slowly made his way through the garden, taking care to cut the five most perfect roses he could find. "As I recall, you told me that the first time I proposed to you, I gave you four roses—one for each year I'd been in love with you.

Well," he said, returning to her side and holding out the blooms, "now I give you five."

Lavinia blushed as she accepted the fragrant flowers. "Nicholas, this really isn't necessary—"

"It most certainly is." His eyes on her face, Nicholas bent his right knee and slowly sank to the ground. "And then you told me that I went down on my knee like this, and said that every day we had been apart, my heart broke a little more, but that every day also brought us closer to the time when we would finally be together. Isn't that right?"

Lavinia's lips curved into a loving smile. "Yes."

"But I said something else, too. Something you forgot to tell me."

Lavinia started. "I did?"

"You forgot to tell me, my darling, that I promised to love you for as long as I was capable of drawing breath, and that I would hold you in my arms until the strength left my body and there were no more sunrises. Do *you* remember that?" he asked with infinite gentleness.

Lavinia stared at him, hardly daring to believe what she was hearing. "Nicholas…?"

"And do you remember what you answered?" Nicholas continued, his smile growing broader by the minute. "You said that—"

"I said that…if you couldn't…hold me any more, there would be no more…need for sunrises. Oh, Nicholas! Your memory!" Lavinia laughed as the tears sprang to her eyes and spilled over her lashes. "It's come back. You've remembered! You've truly remembered!"

"Every last detail, my darling," Nicholas told her, joyfully pulling her into his arms. "Everything about who I am, why I went to France and how much I loved you. But there is something else I have to tell you that is even more important than my memory returning, or how much I used to love you," he went on urgently.

Lavinia's eyes gleamed with emotion. "There is?"

Nicholas's gaze grew infinitely tender as he set her slightly away from him and smiled down into her beautiful blue eyes. "I need to tell you that I love you more than I ever imagined possible. To tell you that, even had my memory not come back, it wouldn't have made any difference. Because I love you, Lavinia. Not for what we had, or what you once meant to me, but because of what you mean to me now. You are the *only* woman I have ever loved, my darling, and you are the only woman I ever will—with or without a memory."

"Oh…Nicholas!"

He kissed her then, tasting the saltiness of tears

mingled with the honeyed sweetness of her lips. He ran his mouth over the softness of her cheek, the smooth line of her jaw, pressing his lips to the fluttering pulse at the base of her throat before returning once more to her lips. He held her as if she were the most precious treasure imaginable, because to him she was a treasure, one more valuable than all the gold and jewels in the world. She was his Lavinia, the woman he had promised to love until there were no more sunrises.

"And now, my lady," Nicholas whispered huskily, "if I haven't forgotten anything else, I shall ask you the question I was told to ask again. Darling Lavinia, will you marry me?"

Lavinia opened her mouth, choking on a sob that abruptly turned into a laugh. "Yes! Oh, yes, please." She tightened her arms around his neck and held him with all the strength she possessed. "And as soon as possible, if you don't mind. Before either one of us has a chance to forget another blessed thing!"

*H*istorical
romance™

SPRING BRIDES

THREE BRIDES AND A WEDDING DRESS
by Judith Stacy

Mail-order bride Anna Kingsley journeys across country – only to find her groom has disappeared. Then his handsome cousin Cade Riker offers her a job as his housekeeper. Will she find her happy ending in his arms…?

THE WINTER HEART *by Cheryl Reavis*

Eleanor Hansen is eager for a fresh start in Wyoming. But she finds a lawless land where revenge rules. Can she convince ranch hand Dan Ingram that love is worth more than any vendetta?

McCORD'S DESTINY *by Pam Crooks*

Juliette Blanchard's future depends on buying rancher Tru McCord's land. But her old flame won't sell unless she meets his demands. Juliette must decide how far she'll go for the chance of a lifetime – and the man of her dreams…

THE GLADIATOR'S HONOUR
by Michelle Styles

A hardened survivor of many gladiatorial combats, Gaius Gracchus Valens's raw masculinity fuels many women's sexual fantasies. Roman noblewoman Julia Antonia knows she should have nothing to do with a man who is little more than a slave, but she is drawn inexorably towards the forbidden danger Valens represents…

On sale 5th May 2006

Available at WHSmith, Tesco, ASDA, Borders, Eason, Sainsbury's and most bookshops

www.millsandboon.co.uk

Don't miss this superb 2-in-1 anthology of linked Regency stories from *New York Times* bestselling author Stephanie Laurens.

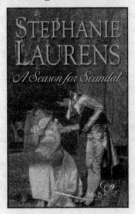

Tangled Reins

Miss Dorothea Darent has no intention of ever getting married, certainly not to the Marquis of Hazelmere. A disreputable scoundrel, he is captivated when they meet. Can he win her heart?

Fair Juno

When the Earl of Merton finds himself playing the knight in shining armour to a damsel in distress, he knows his days as a notorious rake are numbered. But the lady flees the scene without revealing her name...

On sale 21st April 2006

Available at WH Smith, Tesco, ASDA, Borders, Eason, Sainsbury's and all good paperback bookshops

www.millsandboon.co.uk

M&B

2 FREE

BOOKS AND A SURPRISE GIFT!

We would like to take this opportunity to thank you for reading this Mills & Boon® book by offering you the chance to take TWO more specially selected titles from the Historical Romance™ series absolutely FREE! We're also making this offer to introduce you to the benefits of the Reader Service™—

- ★ FREE home delivery
- ★ FREE gifts and competitions
- ★ FREE monthly Newsletter
- ★ Exclusive Reader Service offers
- ★ Books available before they're in the shops

Accepting these FREE books and gift places you under no obligation to buy, you may cancel at any time, even after receiving your free shipment. Simply complete your details below and return the entire page to the address below. You don't even need a stamp!

YES! Please send me 2 free Historical Romance books and a surprise gift. I understand that unless you hear from me, I will receive 4 superb new titles every month for just £3.69 each, postage and packing free. I am under no obligation to purchase any books and may cancel my subscription at any time. The free books and gift will be mine to keep in any case.

H6ZED

Ms/Mrs/Miss/Mr ....Initials ....
                                                                                    BLOCK CAPITALS PLEASE

Surname ....

Address ....

....

....Postcode..........................

Send this whole page to:
UK: FREEPOST CN81, Croydon, CR9 3WZ